4

Declan

CHRIS KENISTON
USA TODAY BESTSELLING AUTHOR

Indie House Publishing

Indie House Publishing

BOOKS BY CHRIS KENISTON

Aloha Series
Aloha Texas
Almost Paradise
Mai Tai Marriage
Dive Into You
Shell Game
Look of Love
Love by Design
Love Walks In
Waikiki Wedding

Surf's Up Flirts
(Aloha Series Companions)
Shall We Dance
Love on Tap
Head Over Heels
Perfect Match
Just One Kiss
It Had to Be You

Honeymoon Series
Honeymoon for One
Honeymoon for Three

Family Secrets Novels
Champagne Sisterhood
The Homecoming
Hope's Corner

ACKNOWLEDGEMENTS

The Farraday family has been a wondrous adventure in can-you-read-faster-than-I-write. Every time I finish a book I'm amazed to discover people like it!

Declan's book has been one heck of a ride. Author Kathy Ivan opened her home to me every afternoon to keep me honest and on schedule. Steve Richards once again explained to me, ever so patiently, how the Dallas police department really works, and what DJ could and couldn't do. Bless Author Angi Morgan for knowing all things Texas Ranger (I may need you soon). I thank all of you for the help along the way. All of you made Declan a much better read.

I especially want to thank all the great new fans who have found me because of the Farradays and faithfully returning fans. It's been an absolute blast reading the reviews and emails. I kid you not even as I write this I am super pumped because of a fantastic review I just saw. Y'all rock. Thank you!

CHAPTER ONE

"The Louisville Slugger strikes again." DJ dropped the receiver into place and pushed back from his desk. "That's the fifth mailbox this week."

Teenage hijinks were one thing, but this was getting totally out of hand. And picking on old Mrs. Peabody this time. Since her husband died, the woman had more than enough imaginary problems, she didn't need real ones. Who knew how long he and his department would have to drive by her house more regularly until she found something new to fret about. With only a few officers besides himself for the small town and the handful of ranches inside the Tuckers Bluff limits, circling Mrs. Peabody's neighborhood all day—and night—wasn't practical, but he'd do it.

Esther, his dispatcher, stuck her arm out. A single pink message slip dangled between her fingers. "You may want to call your brother back."

"Which one?"

"Brooks. I took the call while you were calming down Mrs. Peabody."

DJ looked at the note. *Says he may have saved your day.* "Thanks." A rustling noise near the front door caught his attention, but his cell phone ringing pulled him back. "Farraday."

"If you're coming over you'd better get here sooner than later," Brooks said quickly. "I'm almost done with Christopher Brady."

"Christopher?" More movement out front had him crossing the bullpen toward the window. "What about him?"

"Mom brought him in with a broken arm."

"Oh really?" Christopher was about to learn the hard way, Karma was a bitch.

"Yeah. I'm guessing you had another mailbox go down."

Scanning the street, DJ nodded even though his brother couldn't see him. "Mrs. Peabody."

"If you want my professional opinion, looks like this Brady son isn't taking too well to the attention the twins are getting."

"Yeah, you're probably right. I'll be right over." DJ slid his phone into his pocket and took a step toward the scratching sound coming from the front door and waited. Nothing. Maybe his family was right, he needed a little time off. A break. Tuckers Bluff was no mecca for crime, but sometimes having nothing to do all day was as draining as having too much to do. Though he'd take those long winter days with no sign of trouble anywhere on the horizon and the increased mischief come spring over big city crap any day. Turning to face Esther, the indispensable dispatcher who'd worn a badge long before he'd become a cop, he waited for her to finish her call.

"Yes, ma'am," Esther said with a smile. "I know how you feel." She also nodded even though the caller couldn't see her. "You can be sure I'll remind him." This time Esther chuckled. "I don't know if I'd say that." Her head bobbed a few more times before her eyes rolled and then the smile came back again. "Yes, ma'am, you have a better day now."

"Let me guess," DJ shifted his weight. "Mrs. Peabody."

Esther nodded. "You talk to your brother?"

"On my way now." Almost at the door, another scraping sound drew his attention. Waving to Esther, he took a quick broad step and yanked the door open. "Well."

Resting on his haunches beside one of the old wooden benches flanking either side of the front stoop, with his tail wagging and tongue lolling, a dog who had to be first cousins with a neighborhood wolf sat as contented as any family mascot.

"Hey there." DJ inched forward, not sure how long that tail would keep wagging. He was rewarded with a raised paw. "You shake, do you?" Taking his chances, DJ accepted the proffered paw, pumped it once and then scratched the animal's neck in search of a collar or tags. "You must belong to someone. No stray learns to shake." *Wait a minute.* "I bet you're the fellow who has been popping up all over the place."

DJ would have sworn the dog nodded.

"Don't go anywhere. I know some people who are going to want to check you out." Continuing to scratch the dog's neck, DJ pulled out his cell and called his other brother's office. Came in handy having both a people and animal doctor in the family.

"Animal Clinic, how may I help you?" Becky Wilson's jubilant voice came through his phone and made him smile. The kid was always so happy and perky, just the sound of her voice could put a smile on the Grinch.

"I've got someone here for Adam to check out."

"Well, he's not here. Things were pretty slow so he and Meg took off for some shopping in Butler Springs."

"Dang. I've got *the* dog."

"The dog?" she repeated. "Oh wait. You mean *that* dog?" Her voice kicked up an octave and now he really smiled.

"I think so."

"Cool! Don't let him go. I'm on my way."

Before he could say another word, the line went dead and he decided the Brady boy could wait. It wasn't like DJ didn't know where the family lived. He just really wished Christopher hadn't graduated from TPing houses to destruction of private property. Turning a blind eye wasn't an option and this level of vandalism surpassed the token stern warning.

"Becky's on her way," he explained to the dog. "You're going to like her."

Again the pooch did that head bob that looked like nodding. Spinning around, he leaped up on his hind legs as if he were asking to dance, and then coming back down, shifted to the opposite side, giving DJ a better view of what had been nestled under the old bench behind the fluffy dog.

"Don't tell me someone dumped your puppies here and that's what's brought you out into the open." Keeping one hand on the dog's collar, DJ leaned over, grabbed hold of the cardboard edge and slid the box out into the open. For a split second he thought he was hallucinating. Blinking once and then twice, he shook his head. No hallucination. Squatting down, he reached forward. "Son of a—"

• • • •

Bolting up from her seat, Becky spun around to face her friend and receptionist, Kelly. "Looks like DJ found that mysterious dog. He's got him at the station. I'm running over now."

"Is he hurt?" Like everyone else in town who'd heard about the disappearing dog, Kelly knew some reports had the pup limping. No one liked the idea of an injured animal out on its own.

"We'll see. I'll bring him back. Even if he's not hurt, the poor fellow needs a good home."

"The way he took care of Toni's husband and little Stacey, I'd say he seems to have a protective streak. Maybe your grandmother would like another dog now that you've moved out."

Becky rolled her eyes and fished her keys out of her purse. "Don't give her any ideas." Skirting the edge of the counter, she waved at Kelly. "Be back soon."

"No hurry," Kelly called back.

One of the nicer things about Becky's job was working with one of her best friends and the coolest boss. It didn't hurt any that by working for the eldest Farraday brother, she could keep tabs on Ethan without having to straight out ask about him. Though she saw plenty on social media, she knew there was plenty more that wasn't available for public consumption. And then she tried not to think about the plenty more that not even his family would know of.

The police station was halfway down Main Street. Not a great distance in Tuckers Bluff, but under the circumstances, walking would take too long. Riding down the block in her little pickup, she moved as quickly as possible without drawing too much attention. Of course, she had to take a minute to wave at Burt Larson pulling in some sale barrels from the sidewalk in front of the hardware store. No doubt lugging those things in and out all day is how he managed to keep up with the town gossip. Then the small town code of ethics required her to roll the window down a minute to share a word with Polly closing up the Cut and Curl. "Early day today?"

"Yeah, Mrs. Thorton cancelled her color. Figure it's about time I had an afternoon off."

Becky nodded and waved. "Enjoy."

Most of the storefronts rolled up the welcome mat early during the week, and if she'd waited a few more minutes she'd have probably had to stop for every single proprietor making their way home.

For a place intended to contain lawbreakers, the police station had a very pleasant curb appeal. Becky slid into an open spot in front and then, scurrying past the benches and potted plants to the inset triple glass door, she practically ran inside, only to stop short in the middle of the bullpen.

As expected, DJ stood with a better-than-medium-sized furry gray animal at his feet, but rather than waiting for her in his office, the two were completely fixated on Esther, patting and rocking a baby. "Starting a babysitting service now?" Becky asked.

"Apparently." Esther hummed to the infant curled into her shoulder.

The dog broke free of DJ's hold and loped in Becky's direction.

"Whoa." DJ turned after the dog.

Tail wagging, the pup reached Becky first, plopped his butt in front of her and offered his paw.

"He did that to me too." DJ stopped in front of her, his darkened gaze darting back to the baby.

"So you're a gentleman, are you?" She squatted down and using both hands scratched at the dog's neck and raised her head to look at DJ. "Whose baby?"

"We were just about to find out."

"Find out?" She glanced from DJ to Esther and back.

DJ waved a couple of envelopes at her. "The baby was left here on the stoop in a cardboard box. These came with the bundle." Turning toward his office, the envelopes in one hand, DJ gestured to the dog with the other. "Rin Tin Tin here was standing guard."

"Aren't you a good doggie." She continued scratching behind his ears. "I can't believe anyone from around here would just drop an unprotected baby off on the doorstep." Patting the top of the dog's head, she pushed upright and walked over to Esther. "Girl or boy?"

"Haven't checked. When the chief picked the box up, the poor thing startled awake and Mr. Dad over there handed it off to me so fast you'd have thought the baby was on fire."

Cooing, Becky patted the baby's back. "Aren't babies so sweet?"

DJ tore at an envelope and walked into his office.

The phone rang. Esther looked over to her boss, shook her head, and handed the baby to Becky. "Someone needs to answer that."

"Yes, someone does," DJ called from behind his desk, whipping the folded sheet of paper open.

Becky followed him in. The dog plopped down at the doorway, his gaze on the front door.

Swaying and patting, she rocked the little bundle back to sleep. She loved babies. All children, actually. Ever since she was a little kid herself, she'd dreamed of a pretty white ranch house with a picket-fenced side yard and small children with those strong chiseled Farraday features, deep blue-green eyes, and Ethan's sandy hair. Though with every passing year, the longer Ethan stayed married to the marines, the less Becky's dreams of happily ever after seemed likely to come true. But she wasn't ready to give up on the dream. Not yet. Someday he'd come home and see her for the grown up woman she'd become and then he'd have no choice but to fall head over heels in love with her the same way she'd stumbled into loving him back in first grade. "Who would abandon something so precious?"

"That's what I'm trying to figure out." DJ continued to scan the page in front of him. "All this says is that the few days she and the father spent together were fantastic." He glanced up over the edge of the page. "I'll spare you the, er…intimate details."

Becky looked down in an effort to hide the blush she knew would creep into her cheeks any minute. She could joke and tease about sex with the girls any Friday night, no problem, but surrounded by strong handsome men, or in this case, man, her old fashioned upbringing always came to life.

"Sounds like mama was—is—a bit of a wild child," DJ continued scanning. "Thought maybe it was time to settle down. That getting pregnant even though they'd used precautions was a sign from God." DJ raised his dark brows at that one.

"I'm guessing the novelty wore off pretty quick."

"Yeah." He turned to a second page. "She's just going to drive and stop wherever the bright lights call to her, knows Brittany—"

"So you're a girl." Becky kissed the top of the precious child's head. "I should have known. Such a sweet face."

DJ continued, "The mother knows she'll be better off with a stable family. Family? Sh…oot." DJ blew out a heavy sigh, and closing his eyes, pinched the bridge of his nose. "If the clueless papa already has a family then Daddy Dearest is married. Wonder how well that's going to go over with Mrs. Daddy Dearest."

"Don't know how stable the family can be if Mr. Daddy is stepping out on the Mrs. Does the letter say who Daddy is?"

Shaking his head, DJ set the paper on the desk and pulled out his cell. "Reed, I want you to park yourself at the mouth of Route 9."

"We looking for drunks or speeders at this time of day?" the junior officer asked.

"Neither. You see any car you don't recognize, pull the plates and call me back." DJ disconnected the call and continued scanning the letter.

"You think the mother's not local?"

DJ nodded. "We don't have any place in town for a married man to have a long weekend party that his wife won't find out about."

"Why'd she drop Brittany off here instead of with Daddy?"

"Probably," DJ folded the letter back into the envelope and slid out another sheet, "so that she can't be arrested. Leaving the baby at a safe house in Texas protects her from prosecution."

"I don't call the front stoop very safe."

"Yeah, she probably knew one of us would be coming in or out." He looked up through the glass windows of his office and toward the front door. "This is going to be a mess. Even if we figure out who the father is, I'll have to call in protective services, find a certified foster parent. You know the father's going to want DNA tests and, unlike TV, with the state in charge, that sure as hell won't happen overnight."

From all the rocking in place, even with the conversation, the sweet baby had fallen fast asleep. Becky shifted her weight. "I can help."

DJ unfolded the next paper and looked up at Becky. "You know something I don't?"

She shook her head. "I'm still certified for emergency foster care. Remember Gran's cousin Gert died while visiting a couple of years ago? She had her grandson Chase with her. His mama had been gone a while by then and she'd never told Gert who his daddy was."

"That's right. Y'all had the boy for a couple of months before Social Services found the father."

"We'd have kept him too if Gran hadn't liked the guy. Apparently he didn't even know he had a son."

"Seems there's a lot of that going around." DJ returned his attention to the page in front of him. Like a full moon in fall, his eyes rounded wide until the whites totally surrounded those deep blue orbs.

"What is it?"

His hand fell hard to the table. "This is a birth certificate."

"Good. At least we know who the mother is."

DJ nodded. "We know the father too."

Something in his voice gave her goose flesh. Surely DJ hadn't been the one carousing with strange women. Though now that she thought about it, none of the Farraday men dated the local girls, and she'd have to be a damn fool to think they were all celibate. She swallowed hard and waited for his next words.

"Becky." He sucked in a breath. "It's Ethan."

CHAPTER TWO

So much color drained from Becky's face that DJ almost sprang from his chair to take the baby from her, but instead of loosening her grip, she seemed to hold the infant closer to her chest.

Becky's lips pressed together, then sucking on her upper then lower lip, her mouth finally formed words, "I see."

The two simple words cut through DJ like a precision scalpel. The next time he saw that high-flying brother of his... "You still want me to put you down as foster parent?"

Without taking even a second to think about it, Becky nodded. Smart, sweet, friendly, caring, responsible and willing to take on the baby another woman had made with the man Becky had followed around like a smitten puppy since she was in first grade. Amazing was the only word that came to mind. Damn, his brother was truly a jackass. But now DJ had a new dilemma—if what this woman in the letter said was true, then this wasn't just any abandoned baby, this was a Farraday. Farradays took care of their own. At any cost.

"Do you think Ethan will come home now?" Becky's voice came out so soft and hopeful that the urge to strangle his own brother once again rose up forcefully inside of him like a shaken bottle of cola.

"I don't know." And he honestly didn't. Though he was sure of one thing—not until there was proof Farraday blood ran in this infant's veins could he ask Ethan or any other member of the family to turn their worlds upside down. In some twisted irony, this baby was his job. Yet, whether he liked it or not, with or without proof, his family's lives were about to go on hold for the next few weeks.

"Did the mother leave anything for the baby? Diapers, formula? You said she was in a box. I'm guessing no car seat or carrier?"

"There was a diaper bag with two bottles, a Ziploc bag of powdered formula and a few diapers, but that's it."

"I guess I'm going shopping." Becky rolled back on her heels.

DJ shook his head. "For the moment, *we're* going shopping. Lord knows when the state will get around to reimbursing you. If what the mother says is true and she's Ethan's baby, then there's no way I'm going to let you pick up the tab for my niece." Whoa, did that sound weird. *His niece.*

"I suppose that makes sense." She took a step back and glanced down at the sleeping baby, then trained her gaze on DJ again. "You called her your niece. You think it's true."

"I don't think much of anything right now other than I have a ton of paperwork to fill out, phone calls to make, and all of it can wait until morning, but no matter who she belongs to, this baby needs more than a diaper bag."

Becky nodded. "The Sisters shop?"

Boy, he didn't like that suggestion one bit. Not that rumors wouldn't be flying within the hour regardless, but at the Sisters shop, they'd be broadcast across the county before he finished saying car seat. "I don't see we have any other choice." He took hold of her elbow. "Come on. I'll drive."

In the middle of the bullpen, Becky scanned left and right then back again. "Where's the dog?"

The shock and surprise at discovering the abandoned baby, who might very well be his niece, had completely swept aside any concerns for the stray dog. The stray dog that was now missing. Again. DJ looked to the front door. Latched shut. "Esther, did someone open this door?" The older woman shook her head. "Nope."

"Then where's the dog?"

"Right…" Esther's words fell off, she blinked, looked around and shrugged. "Maybe the door wasn't shut all the way?"

"That has to be it." Becky frowned.

At this moment, DJ would accept any explanation that didn't require burning up more brain cells. "Yeah. That's probably what happened. Pup nudged the door open and the wind slammed it shut."

Becky nodded reluctantly. "I hope he's okay."

At the moment, DJ was pretty sure the dog was in better shape than anyone. At least he'd already done his job protecting the baby, now came the fun part. Securing the kid's future.

Walking down Main Street, Becky kept her attention on the sleeping baby in her arms. "How old is she?"

"According to the birth certificate, two months."

"So that would be..."

"Eleven months ago." He didn't want to make her say out loud what she was thinking. "If my memory serves me right, Ethan was doing some training program around then."

"Air Station Miramar," she mumbled, then chuckled. "Top Gun."

"Not anymore. They moved that to Nevada."

"I know." She looked up. "That whole image just seems to fit Ethan so well. Even when we were little, he and Connor were the daring ones. The risk takers."

"Each with their own passions. For Connor it was horses, for Ethan flying." DJ wasn't going to say this out loud, but the brothers had always razzed Ethan that he was going to become one of those Naval jet jocks who, in dress whites and gold wings, could get a woman into bed anywhere. Truth was, the kid didn't need dress whites or gold wings to pull that off.

"He had his pilot's license before his driver's license," Becky added.

"You remember that?" The second the words were out of his mouth he wished he could take them back. Of course she remembered. She probably knew Ethan's height and weight from birth to his last physical. He glanced sideways to see her smile slip as she nodded. *Kick 'em while they're down, Declan James. Way to go asshat.* DJ came to a stop in front of Sisters. Looking like a boutique from the outside, it was the closest thing the town had to a general store. "As soon as we've picked everything out, I'll run back to the station and bring the car."

Her smile returned. "Works for me."

"You still doing okay? Need me to take her?"

"Nah, she barely weighs more than a sack of sugar."

He had to admit the baby had looked awfully breakable when Esther lifted her out of the box. Taking his time, he shortened his stride to match Becky's. At the door, his mind grappled with whether to be polite and hold the door for her or lead the way taking on the sisters' first barrage of questions. Stepping inside, straddling the doorway, his arm easily extending high over Becky's head, he precariously managed to do both.

"Well what do we have here?" Sister, the sibling shop owner with no qualms about maintaining a decades-old beehive hairdo, came rushing up to Becky and the baby. "I don't recognize this little bundle."

Recognize? DJ didn't know much about babies, but he'd seen enough of them to know at that size they pretty much all looked alike.

Becky smiled and eyed DJ over the now doubled over and cooing older woman.

"She's a ward of the state. Becky's her foster mother." The words came out before his brain had time to filter what he'd said. Something about sweet young Becky and the word mother didn't line up. But holding what might be Ethan's baby in her arms made the choice of words seem less than prudent. Not to mention there was always the possibility that social services would want to place the child somewhere else. That thought had a knot tightening in his gut. He might have to pull in a few favors if it came to that, but this child was not leaving his care.

As the baby got passed from sister to sister and back, Becky and DJ picked out the bare necessities. A time or two DJ noticed Becky lingering a tad too long over a frilly little outfit or a bouncing accessory of some kind or other. With Becky once again rocking in place and the two sisters fussing and making funny voices at the wide awake baby, DJ decided now would be a good time to get his car. "I'll be back in a few minutes with a way to carry all this loot home."

The three women nodded, but no one reacted as though they'd actually heard him. He couldn't blame them, there was something mesmerizing about such a young baby. Including him. *Damn.* This wasn't a crazy kid blowing up a hollow tree stump or even a bunch of unruly teens drunk on watermelon wine. How the hell was he supposed to straighten out this mess?

• • • •

For an abandoned infant, little Brittany was an easy baby. Most of the time she slept. When she did wake up, she barely let out a peep while Becky changed her diaper and then seemed to be more than happy studying the sisters as they took turns feeding her. Having finished almost the whole bottle, Brittany was good eater as well. Why would a woman give up such a sweet little thing?

Once DJ returned with the patrol car, Becky strapped the baby into the new massive car seat. Brittany opened her eyes a moment as though wondering what the heck Becky was doing to her and then fell right back into slumber.

"Need some help?" she asked softly.

His phone at his ear, he shook his head and continued speaking with one of the brothers while loading all the things they'd bought into the trunk. From the front passenger seat, Becky sat on her hip keeping one eye on the baby and the other on DJ. For a few minutes, she let her imagination run away with her. Changing DJ's dark locks to lighter, she pictured Ethan happily shopping for his family. Instead of certified foster care, she was the mother. Rather than seeing DJ look over at the child with questions in his eyes, she pictured Ethan looking at her with unparalleled love and devotion. Same dream she'd had since she was six years old. She was all set to design their happy home in her mind for the millionth time when DJ's door opened.

"That was Brooks. He's going to corral the others and call an emergency brothers' meeting. I don't want to tell my father and Aunt Eileen just yet. Not until we work a few things out and there's no point bringing Grace into it from Dallas."

"She'll be pissed." Becky knew her other best friend very well. Always the Lucy Ricardo character egging Kelly and Becky into all sorts of trouble, Grace also leaned toward running the show. A reason why law school was a great fit for her, even if she claimed the only reason she'd chosen it after college was because a JD was the fastest way to a doctorate salary.

The way DJ looked at her, she wasn't sure if he was reconsidering the brother's decision or if maybe she'd put her blouse on backwards this morning. "You always did have my sister's back," he finally said. "We'll just have to deal with Grace when the time comes."

"You do know I talk to her all the time? Kelly too? She's going to find out the baby."

DJ winced. "Of course, you're right, but I'm not dealing with speaker phones or chat time tonight. Let's figure out where we stand and then we can bring Sis in."

All Becky could do was nod. Regardless of the outcome of the family gathering, there was little Grace could do about anything hundreds of miles away in Dallas. "My apartment is almost ready for company."

"About that." DJ put the car in gear and backed out of the space. "I've been thinking—"

"Stop." She cut him off, shaking her head.

Turning the car onto Main Street he glanced in her direction.

"Don't say it."

DJ lifted a questioning brow.

"We're not passing this baby off to someone else." Angling herself to face DJ, she leaned against the door and crossed her arms. "Tell me one thing."

Returning his attention to the road, DJ nodded.

"If this weren't Ethan's baby—"

"Alleged baby," DJ corrected.

"Fine. Alleged baby. Would you try to find a different foster parent?" She watched DJ's lips press tightly together and his jaw muscles tighten. She also saw the moment he'd made up his own mind.

"No," was all he said.

"I thought not. No matter what you or anyone else in this town thinks, I'm perfectly capable of taking care of anyone's baby."

"That was never the problem." DJ reached the point where he'd have to continue to his place or turn for hers. Glancing at the rearview mirror, he stopped in the middle of the street and faced her. "Towns talk."

"Tell me something I don't know."

"If you don't want people carrying on about your feelings for Ethan—"

"Alleged feelings," she corrected and was glad to see that bring a smile to DJ's face. She knew damn well how she felt about Ethan, but that didn't mean she hadn't spent most of her life convincing the town otherwise.

"Alleged feelings, then it might be best for us to figure out another solution. If I wait to report—"

"Don't go there." Becky held her hand up at DJ, palm out. "First, you're a respected and fair man, Declan James Farraday. Don't start breaking the rules now because of me."

"It's not—"

"And second," she said over him. "You don't think not letting me care for this child isn't going to make the town talk? Surely you didn't move away for so long that you could have forgotten everything is everyone's business in this town and if it isn't, they'll find a way to make it so. Heck, if they could, they'd make me the mother."

DJ swallowed a smile. "I suppose it's a good thing you haven't put on any weight lately."

"See." She uncrossed her arms and turned forward. "Take us home."

CHAPTER THREE

It had taken only a few minutes to redirect everyone to Becky's new apartment instead of to Brooks and Toni's house. Becky made sense. There would be no protecting her from gossip no matter how the situation was handled. The first thing he unloaded was the travel crib. "Where do you want this?"

"I suppose in my room." Becky set the infant carrier on the floor and led the way.

Up until about the time Adam and Meg married, Becky had been living with her grandmother Dorothy. It had taken a few weeks of battling not only her grandmother, but the entire Tuckers Bluff Ladies Afternoon Social Club to get the stamp of approval on moving into her own apartment. The final acquiescence came when Adam chimed in how helpful it would be having someone he trusted living over his animal clinic now that he'd move into Meg's remodeled Victorian. Of course the discounted rental rate hadn't hurt her case any.

Becky ran ahead and pushed an old rocker aside to make space in the corner of her room. "Right here will be good. I'll get a knife to open the box."

"No need." DJ pulled a Swiss Army knife from his pocket and sliced the tape open then dumped the contents out of the box. Becky reached in front of him and, squatting, unzipped the case surrounding the folded contraption. Her pants tightened nicely around her backside and DJ found himself taking a mental step back.

"This is really easy." She tossed the outer case aside and, pushing herself upright, spread open the one-piece crib.

"Interesting." Despite the ladies assuring him at Sisters that this brand was the simplest on the market, DJ had expected the some-assembly-required rule of projects-from-hell to come into play.

"Easy peasy." She smiled up at him, bending over and pressing down on the middle, once again displaying a surprisingly well-rounded bottom.

The hospital scrubs that Becky always wore for work gave no inkling of the figure hidden underneath. As a matter of fact, her normal attire tended toward baggy sweatshirts over blue jeans, denim pants standard for anyone in ranch country. More than once through the years, he'd caught a snippet of conversation between his sister and her friends where Becky would bemoan having the shape of a teenage boy. Right about now DJ would be willing to testify on a stack of bibles in any court of law that not a thing about her backside resembled any teenage boy he'd ever known.

"All we have to do now," Becky said as she snapped an overlapping side into place, "is make sure these are secure."

"Let me." Grateful for something to do with his hands, DJ took over securing the snaps. Even if Becky hadn't loved his brother for most of her life, the thoughts suddenly running through his mind were totally and completely inappropriate. Becky was one of his sister's best friends. His baby sister.

"Great." Spinning about, she grabbed another section of crib still in the case. "Now we add this."

"Okay." He nodded, redirecting his thoughts to the project at hand. "Now this is making more sense."

Together they snapped another higher section in place, inserted support rods and finally added a padded section to give the baby more comfort.

"We don't want the padding too soft." Becky stepped back and, smiling, gave the newly assembled infant bed a nod of approval. "We done good."

Her arm shot out and DJ instinctively grabbed hold to shake. The soft hand felt so unexpectedly fragile in his that he almost withdrew his hand. When she pumped his arm once and pulled away, he lingered somewhere between relief and regret at the loss.

"Okay." She rubbed her hands at her sides and looked around the room. "I'd better get Brittany."

"Yes. Right." On her heels, DJ glanced around as he crossed the small room, his eyes falling on the large bed in the center piled high with pillows and framed with an old brass headboard. His mind instantly shot places it had no business going. Little sister's best friend, he reminded himself, and then he decided as soon as this baby business was over he was taking a day off and going to Butler Springs. It was way past time he let off a little steam.

In the middle of the living room, Becky bent over to lift Brittany from the carrier.

Okay—a lot of steam.

• • • •

Even though Becky wasn't part of the family, every Farraday brother in the room insisted she stay and participate in the conversation.

"So what do you think?" Adam held the birth certificate in his hand. "Does this ring legit, or is she just looking for an easy mark to take on her kid?"

"No clue." DJ hefted a tired shoulder. "Didn't see her."

"Doesn't matter, you can't judge a book by its cover," Toni chimed in, squeezing Brooks' hand. "Or in this case, a mother, had you seen her."

"Doesn't strike me that we need much to conclude whoever she is, she's a lousy mother." Meg leaned back against her husband Adam. "Really lousy mother."

"Not sure I agree." Brooks set the note he'd been reading down on the table in front of him. "I've seen a lot of women who shouldn't take care of their own kids, didn't want to take care of their own kids, but did. The results were pretty grim. If this woman, whoever she is, left the baby with a caring family, that may be the most praiseworthy thing she could have done."

Becky didn't like the look that had washed over Brooks' face. Tucker Falls was no Garden of Eden, lots of bad stuff happened to good people, but she was pretty sure nothing compared to the ugly things coming through the ER of a big city hospital. And she suspected all of them had just flashed before Brooks' eyes.

"What's it going to take to know the truth?" Connor asked. Rather than ask Aunt Eileen to baby-sit Stacey and risk her asking too many questions, he and Catherine decided she'd stay home. The way he looked at his brothers and their wives, Becky got the feeling he missed having Catherine at his side. Funny how quickly a man could change once he met the right woman.

Meanwhile, Finn, the youngest brother who'd ridden into town with Connor, hadn't said a word the entire time. He'd read the note and the birth certificate and then passed it on to the next brother beside him. He'd listened to the comments and questions and hadn't made a single gesture or sound to give an impression of what he thought.

The scene before her almost had Becky laughing. All the brothers, ranging somewhere between six foot and six foot four, were imposing figures. The strong Farraday genes had taken root in every one of them. There would be no denying these men were related. And though Adam was the eldest and Finn the youngest, for some time now his words seemed to always be the deciding factor. She had a feeling this wasn't going to be any different.

"If we let the county handle the DNA evidence," DJ said, "it could take six weeks. Or more."

Adam winced, Brooks nodded, Connor shook his head and Finn merely took the information in.

"We could go private," Brooks added.

DJ nodded. "We could. But unlike TV where DNA results are in by morning, even if we use a private lab they'll need days, and the good ones that can do it in days are backlogged."

"Agreed," Brooks sighed. "But even if it takes one week, that's better than months."

Finn looked to his brother, the police chief. "Have you reached out to Ethan?"

The four other brothers snapped around to face him. Clearly the collection of blank expressions meant that the thought hadn't occurred to any of them. With a nod, Finn pulled out his phone, swiped at his screen, ran his finger across it and slid it back into his pocket.

"He mentioned something at the wedding about being out of touch soon." Brooks looked to Finn.

"I remember," Finn said in his normally soft tone, "but still, the best person to let us know if he was anywhere near this woman eleven months ago would be Ethan."

All heads bobbed.

"It might be really early wherever he is," Meg contributed.

Adam shrugged and smiled. "It's not like the Marine Corps sleeps in."

Meg chuckled. "No. I suppose not."

"Definitely not." Both former marines, Connor and DJ echoed.

"Which brings us back full circle." DJ leaned forward, resting his forearms on his knees. "State laws have to be followed. I have to report the abandoned infant and the only way to keep control of the situation is to place her with an emergency care certified foster parent here in town."

Becky raised her hand and wiggled her fingers. "That would be me."

"Really?" Meg said, then quickly covered her mouth with her hand. "Sorry, just—"

"Don't worry about it," Becky cut her off. One of the downsides of looking like she was still a teen was that some people had a hard time believing she could do an adult's job. The bright side, she kept telling herself, would come in about thirty years if she still looked half her age. "I'll get even at forty."

Meg chuckled, a few others smiled, and DJ went back to the conversation. "Becky has changed residence since she was certified but the idea is that an emergency parent is ready at the drop of a hat to take in a child and, as you can see, we've made her ready. I do think it sucks that we have to impose on her or anyone else for Farraday business—"

"*If* it's Farraday business," Adam interrupted.

"Exactly," DJ continued, "and that's our dilemma."

"Can't we just take the baby to the ranch and tell the county she's with Becky?" Toni asked. "I mean, if the problem is you want the baby at the ranch."

"I'm not so sure I do." DJ leaned forward, and a little like a choreographed scene from the musical their mother had loved enough to name them after, the other brothers inched forward also. "I don't even think I want to tell Dad and Aunt Eileen until we know for sure."

"She'll skin our hides for keeping this a secret." Connor pushed back in his seat again. "Twice."

DJ nodded. "Agreed, but do you really want her fussing over a new baby and then have to give it back?"

"So you think this woman is lying?" Adam leaned back this time.

"That's not the point." Brooks sighed. "Aunt Eileen will also start stewing over how many other Farraday grandbabies has Ethan been sprouting that we don't know about until the possibilities drive her crazy with worry."

"Exactly," DJ said. "Besides, we don't need the county paying a surprise visit and finding the baby not with Becky."

"What can they do?" Connor asked.

Finn leaned forward. "Doesn't matter. We do this the right way. Becky keeps the baby." He dipped his chin in her direction. "Thank you."

She smiled back at him. Such a nice guy.

"But we need to make other arrangements as well," Finn continued. "Babies need a lot of attention and care and Becky has a full-time job. One that requires her getting some sleep at night."

So enamored with the little baby, Ethan's baby, she hadn't given much thought to how different caring for an infant would be from caring for her distant cousin. "I suppose I could move back to Gran's for a while." Though she really, really didn't want to do that, she also had to be practical.

"We're not going to chase you out of your home." Adam was the first to shake his head, then he glanced at Meg and she shrugged. "Are you opposed to letting one of us sack out on the sofa?"

"Well," she glanced at her secondhand sofa. Though comfortable for her, she couldn't picture it holding Adam's or Brooks' over six-foot frame. But again, she knew it would be better taking turns at night if anyone was going to get any real rest. "I suppose that will be fine."

Brooks and Toni exchanged a round of silent communication and Becky felt like she was waiting to see who drew the short straw. Who would have to upheave their lives to help her with the baby. A big part of her wanted to say don't bother, she'd be fine, but the truth was, she had no idea how well she would handle single motherhood.

"I happen to have an in with Becky's boss," Meg smiled. "Nice fellow. I think it's safe to say the baby can stay at the clinic during the day. This will make it easy for everyone to chip in. I don't really have to stick around the B&B once breakfast is over."

"Of course you do," Toni spoke up. "You don't want guests roaming about without a homeowner."

Meg shook her head. "I've only got that one couple and they're out all day long antique scavenging."

"I think the point is that we're all willing to help," Finn chimed in. "Though frankly, if this isn't resolved quickly, it's going to be hard for me to get away from the ranch without Aunt Eileen and Dad asking a lot of questions."

"Ditto," Connor said.

"Meg is right." Adam winked at his wife. "The baby can come to work. That won't be a problem and we can cover for you in the morning if you need some extra sleep. But Connor and Finn bunking out won't work at all."

Becky bobbed her head. This was starting to get a bit more complicated than she'd first considered. The only corner not heard from was DJ. He'd sat rather quietly. His gaze darted over to the bedroom door where the baby slept, the silence broken by tiny sounds signaling she wouldn't be sleeping for long. He looked around to Becky. "I was only six when Grace was born, but I remember finding Aunt Eileen in the hall late at night, and looking dead to the world most of the day."

"Dad was having a hard time, he wasn't much help the first few months," Adam said.

DJ's gaze shifted to the room where the tiny cry had grown stronger. "She's going to be waking up every few hours, isn't she?"

"That's how it's supposed to work. Feed, change, and back to sleep." Becky shifted a little closer to the door, eager to cradle the bundle again, but knowing the longer Brittany slept between feedings the better for everyone.

"You're going to need help when she starts screaming at two in the morning." DJ wasn't asking.

"She might sleep through the night." *And pigs might fly.*

"No." DJ shook his head and stood. "Until paternity can be conclusively determined to the satisfaction of the county, looks like you've got yourself a roommate."

CHAPTER FOUR

What the hell had DJ gotten himself into? Over the next short while, the family got totally distracted passing the now wide-awake and very hungry baby around. Meg felt certain she had the strong Farraday chin. Toni agreed the blue eyes resembled any one of the brothers, which made each of them, married or single, squirm just a bit.

While everyone pretended having a baby around was no big deal, nothing out of the ordinary, DJ took advantage to make a run to his place for a change of clothes and some sleeping gear. As much as Becky might appreciate the help in the middle of the night, he didn't think she'd want him running around in his boxers. An overnight bag packed and ready to go with a few necessities, he put in a quick call to his oldest brother.

"What?"

"Nice way to answer the phone."

"Don't give me grief. If it's bad news, let it rip."

"No. Just checking on who's still at Becky's and if I have time to stop at the station."

"Oh yeah, everyone is still here." Adam's tone softened from the gruff way he'd answered the phone, a hint of humor coming through. "It's been decided that Brooks has the most immediate need for baby training. He's on his second diaper."

"Why second?"

"Don't ask," Adam laughed heartily.

"Okay. I'll just take a minute and then I'll be right over."

"Take your time. No one seems to be in any hurry."

Disconnecting the call, DJ figured that was probably a good thing. Becky would be getting all the help she needed for now. When he got to her place, he'd have to be the second Farraday brother in baby training. What he knew about babies began and ended with the limited emergency care he'd learned from the department. But then again, how hard could changing a diaper be?

Pulling into his spot in front of the station, he looked up and down the street. Nice quiet night. Typical in this town. Most nights passed without a single call. It's why any emergency calls after midnight came to whoever was on duty's cell phone. Tonight, Reed would be patrolling the area. Good man. DJ'd been lucky to get someone as sharp as him to join the tiny Tuckers Bluff police force.

If DJ wanted to nail down the proud papa, he'd better get moving. Sitting out here in his car studying the empty streets wasn't going to help uncover anything new about Brittany. Inside, a single bullpen light was on. The coffee pot was turned off, but still warm. Reed must have been by recently. Taking his place behind his desk, DJ logged onto the computer. Pulling a list of private labs for DNA testing, he scrolled through data, ratings, complaints, and when he reached the bottom of the list he didn't have any better idea of who to trust for a speedy and accurate report.

Continuing to scroll through searches and pages, he pulled out his phone and hit the one number he knew would have answers.

The phone picked up on the second ring. "Can't live without me?"

"Yeah, that's it. Tell Sharla to pack up, you're moving to Texas."

Luke "Brooklyn" Chapman chuckled on the other end. "I couldn't get her to pack up and move to Hawaii, Texas doesn't stand a chance."

This time DJ laughed. "You may have a point."

Brooklyn's tone dropped, "What's up?"

"Need to prove—or disprove—paternity. Fast."

"I see." Brooklyn waited a beat. "You?"

"That would be too easy. Ethan." Another silent beat. "The last of us still in the Corps."

"The pilot." Brooklyn remembered. "Pregnant mother or baby?"

"Baby."

"And the mother doesn't have a problem with a paternity test?"

"Wouldn't know. She left the baby on my doorstep."

"Yours?"

"I'm guessing flying to the Middle East was too much trouble." Though if this baby was Ethan's, DJ should be thankful the mother took the time to bring it all the way to Texas and didn't just abandon her on the closest doorstep. "I need a reputable lab to process DNA sooner than later. The county will take forever and frankly, if she's Ethan's, I want to keep as much of this out of the databases as possible."

"Don't blame you on that one. What do you want from me?"

"Got any pull at a private lab that can put a rush on this?"

"Sure do. You got samples?"

"Baby won't be a problem. Ethan, maybe. Thought I'd check at the ranch. See if he left a hairbrush or toothbrush when he came home for Adam's wedding."

"If you don't, there's always the repository."

DJ swallowed a grin. If Brooklyn could access the Department of Defense's DNA repository for military servicemen, the guy was even better connected than DJ had thought. "Will let you know."

"Expect instructions on where to send the samples and I'll take care of it from there."

"Thanks, appreciate it."

"No problem. And if you ever get tired of the Texas heat, we've got plenty of ocean breezes, beautiful babes, and need for guys with your savvy."

"Good to know. I'll keep that in mind."

Brooklyn let out a loud burst of laughter. "In other words, don't hold my breath. What's she look like?"

"Excuse me?"

"I know you're devoted to the family, but when a guy turns down beaches *and* babes that fast, there's usually only one good reason."

"Sorry to disappoint you. No woman in my life." The way he kept noticing Becky this evening, not as the extra kid at the house or the love-struck teen following Ethan around like a rescued puppy, but as an attractive woman, DJ definitely needed a woman of his own in his life.

"Hmm, if you say so."

An image of Becky rocking Brittany and asking if DJ thought Ethan might come home replayed in his mind. Any man would kill for a smart and beautiful woman like her to be so devoted to him. And not once had Ethan ever shown any interest in Becky other than that of another kid sister. How did his brother turn out to be such a jackass?

• • • •

"They really should consider just putting an X on either side so we know where to place the tabs." Still smiling over his multiple attempts to balance the diaper on the tiny squirming baby, Brooks placed his hand along his new wife's back and ushered her forward. "At least the last one fit and she's sleeping peacefully now."

"You did great." Her hand on her mouth, Becky did her best to hide her own laughter. She'd never considered the possibility that changing a diaper could be such an ordeal.

"Liar, liar pants on fire," Toni shot back, laughing herself. "I'll have to bring him by for more practice or buy stock in Proctor and Gamble."

"Hey," Adam raised both hands palms up in an awkward shrug, "it's not our fault no one ever asked us guys to babysit. You gals have the upper hand."

"Are you saying we're only better at babies?" Meg, Adam's wife of only a few months, stared at him patiently.

Shaking his head, Adam smiled at his wife. "You, my dear, are brilliant at everything."

"Chicken." Meg leaned in and kissed his cheek. "But I love you."

Behind his wife's back, Brooks shot his older brother a thumbs up and Becky almost lost it. Watching the two brothers go from the most eligible bachelors in town to devoted husbands was... sweet. Watching them backpedal most of the evening to save their sex lives was sheer entertainment.

The sound of footfalls on the steps carried into the apartment. Already by the door, Brooks opened it fully, letting DJ inside.

"We were wondering if you were going to make it back before the next diaper change." Adam stepped up beside Brooks. "We're just leaving."

"Finn and Connor already gone?" DJ dropped a gym bag on the floor by the doorway.

"Yep," Adam said. "They were out the door on your heels. Morning chores won't wait for family problems."

"That they won't." DJ hugged his sisters-in-law and slapped the elder brothers on the back. Closing the door behind the last of the visitors, he retrieved his bag from the floor. "Where shall I keep this?"

Becky glanced around the small apartment. While the others were dealing with the diaper and warming Brittany's bottle, she'd taken a few minutes to make space for DJ. "For now just set it down anywhere. I cleared out a couple of drawers for you so you don't have to live out of a suitcase. When the baby wakes up we'll move you in."

DJ's eyes widened slightly before he nodded. "I don't want to put you out."

"You're not. I've needed to cull the excess for a while. I mean, how many t-shirts does a gal need any way?"

"Trick question?" he asked with a smile.

Becky shook her head. "I didn't know how much space you would need in the bathroom. It's not very big, but—"

"A place for my toothbrush is fine."

Leading the way down the hall, she paused at the linen closet, snatched a towel and continued into the bathroom, trying to ignore the sense of a strong healthy male following closely behind her. She hadn't done any real entertaining since she'd moved in. Certainly not any men. But just knowing six foot plus of a Farraday male stood behind her suddenly made her spacious apartment seem stiflingly small.

Standing in the bathroom doorway, she pointed to the left side of the sink. "Like I said, I didn't know how much space you'd need. I hope that's enough."

DJ scanned the tiny space and then flashed a broad smile that made his eyes sparkle an amazing shade of midnight blue. "You really are terrific. Thanks."

Heat burned the inside of her cheeks. Not that she hadn't heard similar words before, but when they came from her grandmother or her boss, they didn't sound quite so...nice. At a sudden loss for what to say next, she spun around and pointed toward the living room. "You didn't eat much earlier—"

"Neither did you."

Those blue eyes twinkled down on her. Like Ethan and Adam, DJ was at least a foot taller than she was and all three had the blue eyes. Only Brooks and Grace had the Irish green. But somehow she didn't remember Ethan's shade of blue being quite so...intense. If anyone had told her that DJ could read her thoughts with those baby blues, now she might believe them. "I wasn't really hungry then."

"But you are now?"

She nodded. When Brooks arrived earlier this evening with a couple of his wife's pizzas, announcing serious family meetings required comfort food, Becky hadn't felt much like eating. Now that things were more settled, her stomach demanded sustenance. "Shall I heat you a slice?"

"Or two." His smile broadened and Becky almost tripped over her own feet.

"Easy." Strong fingers wrapped around her arm and the eyes that had sparkled with amusement darkened and bore into her with concern and...something she couldn't quite identify. "You'd better sit down. I'll heat the pizza."

"I can—"

Easing his grip on her arm, he shook his head. "You've worked all day and dealt with a baby all night. I can heat up pizza. Promise." Taking a slow step back, he didn't move any further until she nodded and took a seat on the sofa.

The strangest sensation thrummed from her arm to her fingertips and back. With a shake of her hand, she decided her arms were most likely not used to carrying a little baby for hours. "Finding everything?" The open kitchen allowed her to easily keep an eye on DJ and the TV, not that she was really watching the TV.

"What's to find?" He reached for the stack of paper napkins. "Plates, napkins. Can't miss the oven."

She chuckled at his sense of humor, something she'd rarely gotten the chance to see.

"Would you like something to drink?"

Hands at her side, she was about to push off the sofa.

"Don't get up. What would you like?"

She eased herself back down. "Just water would be nice."

"One glass of water coming up." A few seconds later he appeared in front of her. A dishtowel over his arm, he presented her the paper plate and plastic glass with the finesse of a maître D at a fancy restaurant.

"Thank you." She took a bite of the warm slice and groaned with delight. "Oh, wow."

"Yeah." DJ took a seat in the nearby chair. "I detect a lot of extra workouts in our future with Toni in the family."

"Mm hm." Becky chewed another tasty morsel. "They seem really happy."

DJ swallowed. "It's a bit startling getting used to, not one, but two new sisters, soon to be three."

"I like how y'all do that."

"Do what?"

"I've noticed you and the others often refer to Meg and Toni not as in-laws but as sisters."

"Well, they are." He shrugged and took another bite. "At least they are now. They're as much a Farraday as my mom was."

"I wish I'd gotten a chance to know her."

A seriousness took over DJ's face. "Some days I wonder how different things might be had she never passed on. I mean, we had a good life. You know that."

"I do," Becky agreed.

"Aunt Eileen was wonderful, but I still wonder what would have been if Mom were still here. Would any of us be any different? Would we have moved on to other careers, choices?"

Becky considered his words. "I bet not much different."

"Why?" He set his plate down in front of him.

"Well, take this baby. She'll be raised in a small town with a huge family for moral support and plenty of old-fashioned values. If she were raised in a city with no extended family and a 'live and let live' attitude, she'd grow up to be a totally different person."

"And your point?"

"I don't think your upbringing would have been very different with your mom. Maybe she would have handled a situation or two a little differently than your aunt would have, but you'd have still grown up on a ranch with chores and family and responsibilities. Children develop their baser values and character by the time they're four. When your mom died you were…?"

"Six."

"You were well on your way to you."

DJ picked the plate up again. "Brooks is right. We should be thanking that woman for bringing Brittany here and not dumping her someplace else."

"Considering we're not around the corner from San Diego, absolutely." Becky reached for another slice. "Did you always want to be a cop?"

"I wanted to be an Indian." DJ flashed a sly grin at her. "But the pay wasn't all that great."

"Ha ha. Cowboys and Indians." Becky shook her head.

DJ balanced an empty plate on his knee. "Actually, not always. For a lot of years, I thought I'd be a rancher like Dad. By the time we were teens, the military was a duty as much as the ranch. Everything after that simply fell into place. What about you? No dreams of being a prima ballerina? First female president?"

"Oh that's rich." Becky almost spit with laughter. "Me and my two left feet wouldn't last a week on stage. As far as first female president, that's Grace's thing. I was always all about the animals. If I brought home one more stray or injured animal, I think my folks would have sold me to the gypsies."

"Aunt Eileen probably said that a time or two about Adam."

"We're well suited." For a split second she thought she saw his eyes spark and narrow before a curtain of calm descended with a nod. Not sure what to make of the unexpected weight that seemed to have settled around them, she pushed to her feet and reached for his empty glass. "Let me--"

"Would you--?" Great minds think alike. DJ stood and reached for his glass at the same time, their fingertips touching from opposite sides of the glass.

Matching smiles bloomed, and Becky was the first to release her hold on the glass. "My turn to get the drinks."

"I didn't know we were taking turns."

"Thought that's why you're here?"

DJ's one brow rose higher than the other and Becky decided that was definitely the sexiest brow she'd ever seen. Instantly, drawing back both her thoughts and where she stood, she shook her head. It was one thing to drool over the Farraday genes on a Friday girl's night, but so another thing when one of those Farradays was two feet in front of you and every touch made your fingers tingle.

The beginning sounds of Brittany waking up drifted from the bedroom and DJ's hold on the paper plate in front of him tightened. "How long do we wait?"

"A little bit more. She's just stirring. It's better to let her sleep as long as she can so that she sleeps through the night sooner than later."

Stacking her plate on his, DJ walked to the kitchen. The playful banter had silenced. The casual man behind the uniform she'd begun to get a glimpse of was gone, replaced by a man with a dutiful purpose. The man she'd come to know most of her adult life.

Several minutes passed before Brittany made more noises, this time a little louder. "Now?" he asked.

"Yeah," she muttered. "All set?"

On his feet already, DJ straightened his shoulders. "No." He shook his head and sucked in a deep breath. "But when the hell has that ever made a difference?"

CHAPTER FIVE

No big deal, DJ told himself. He could do this. He could handle a few days in close quarters with the beautiful girl in love with his brother and he could certainly handle one little baby. And wasn't that one hell of a new problem. Brittany was so tiny. Jumping out of a highflying helicopter or wrestling with a drug-crazed suspect was preferable to handling such a delicate little being. "What if I hurt her?"

Becky smiled and walked past him into the room and up to the portable crib. "She's more sturdy than you think. Let me change her diaper real quick." Brittany fussed more loudly as Becky stripped away the moist diaper and deftly strapped a new one in place. Pulling down the nightwear in one swift movement over the baby's kicking feet, Becky scooped the little girl up against her shoulder. "The trick is to keep one hand under her head and then snuggle her against you right away."

Nodding, DJ followed Becky back into the kitchen. The whole time she made tsking noises at the baby and patted her back. That seemed to work at first, but by the time they'd actually made it into the kitchen, Brittany was squirming and mewling like a pissed-off kitten.

"Here." Becky whirled around, and in another swift maneuver held the baby out to him. "You take her while I heat the bottle."

Where Becky held the baby in two hands, DJ was pretty sure he could crush the tiny thing in only one of his. "Maybe I should warm the bottle. What do I do?"

"Nonsense. Hold out your hands."

Like a good marine used to taking orders, he did as he was told. Holding his hands out in front of him, palms up, he wondered why he'd signed up for this duty. The next thing he knew, the lightweight infant was fully resting on his palms.

"See. That wasn't so hard. Sway or rock her, or if you want you can hold her against you. I'll have that bottle warmed in a second."

Not quite sure how to get the baby closer without smothering her in his shoulder, DJ found himself holding his arms steady in front of him and bobbing her up and down. Squinty little eyes suddenly opened wide and stared up at him. Brittany seemed as surprised to have him holding her as he was. "Hi, there," he whispered the only words that came to mind.

"You're doing great," Becky said over her shoulder.

"You think so?" he asked, never shifting his focus from the tiny baby. "You're being awfully good to me," he told the infant.

"Keep talking. You have a very soothing voice."

"I do?" His gaze shot over to Becky in time to see her cheeks flush bright red.

"I mean to the baby."

"Oh." Of course. It was stupid of him to think he had any effect on Becky. The kid, well maybe not kid, was lock, stock and barrel in love with Ethan.

Becky came up beside him, baby bottle in hand. "Do you want to feed her?"

He shook his head a bit more vehemently than he should have. "I'd better watch you first."

Her shoulders shook with laughter. "Okay. But it's not hard. Really it isn't." Taking the baby from him, she cradled Brittany in the nook of her elbow and tickled the baby's lips with the nipple end of the bottle.

The tiny mouth latched onto the rubbery tip and chunky baby cheeks began moving as she eagerly sucked in her late night dinner.

"It's not like I've never seen a baby animal latch onto its mama or had to bottle feed a calf or foal, but this, this is amazing."

More than once in his life he'd seen a baby bottle-fed, but he'd never really watched this carefully.

"I know. It never gets old." As Becky looked down at the infant with such tenderness, two things crossed DJ's mind. First, how the hell could this baby's mother leave her in a damn box on a doorstep protected by nothing but a stray dog? And second, why the hell did such an amazing young woman's heart have to belong to his brother?

• • • •

The sight before Becky had been so precious, so adorable, so sweet, that she'd taken much longer to prepare the bottle than she'd actually needed. She still couldn't make up her mind who had been more in awe, DJ with the baby or the baby with DJ. Both were mesmerized. Brittany with her tiny mouth opened in a perfect O and her crystal-blue eyes following DJ's slightest movement. And DJ's whole body had bobbed and swayed with his arms, all the time his voice coming out soft and lilting. Too precious to see a tough guy like him handling such a young infant. She wouldn't have expected there to be so much tenderness in a man like DJ. Always the tough guy exterior. Probably bolstered by the uniform and show of strength. Whatever woman finally snagged this Farraday brother was in for some very pleasant surprises once the lights went out.

Good grief. First she noticed sexy eyebrows and now her mind played with steamy adult nights between the sheets. Lord, she needed to get a grip. And go on a date. A real one. If only Ethan would just come home and stay home, maybe then she could finally catch his eye. She glanced down at the baby in her arms and bet whoever Brittany's mom was, she probably had an hourglass figure. After all, the mother hadn't had any trouble at all catching Ethan's eye.

"You okay?" DJ frowned at her.

"Yeah, fine."

"You stopped smiling."

"Was I smiling?"

He bobbed his head.

"Just thinking."

"Yeah. My mom would call that contemplating the immortality of the crab." He leaned back against the wall, ankles crossed, oozing that Farraday charm. "I keep hoping my phone is going to ding and let me know that Ethan's answered any one of a dozen messages and can straighten this whole mess out."

Becky nodded. She didn't communicate with Ethan often. Just enough to keep in touch, and not enough to fuel town gossip, but even she knew he was offline. Recently, Ethan had warned the family it might be a short while before he could access a good connection again. She knew that was code for he had a job, a mission, or whatever the military called it when he'd be flying into dangerous places with strong determined men, and with the grace of God, would also fly everyone home safe and sound again. But now wasn't the time to dwell on that. Not that there was ever a good time to think about the people we love being in harm's way. Tugging the bottle away from the bundle in her arms and shifting a cloth rag onto her shoulder, she set Brittany against it and, standing up, patted the baby's back. "You want to try the next round?"

"Next round?"

"Babies need to be burped to make sure they don't get gassy tummies, then they get fed again." She stepped closer to him.

"Gassy tummies?" DJ smiled. "Is that official medical terminology?"

Becky smiled back. "Absolutely." Not leaving him any room to make excuses, she slid the burp rag out from under the baby, laid it on DJ's shoulder and, faster than she thought possible, passed the infant off to him. "You try it. Pretend she's a football."

Arms crossed, Becky tried not to smile at the wide-eyed shock on DJ's face as he realized the baby had been passed off to him, and shifting his gaze from the infant to his shoulder, looked totally befuddled. Placing her hands against Brittany's back, Becky urged DJ to ease the baby forward until she snuggled comfortably against him. It took a few seconds for the tension keeping him stiff to release and his muscles to relax.

"You need to pat her back so she burps," Becky suggested softly.

DJ tapped the baby so lightly, Becky wasn't even sure he was making contact.

"She won't break. You'll have to do better than that," she urged.

Very slowly, DJ added pressure with each pat until the tiny baby let out a belch worthy of a beer chugging frat boy. The only thing larger than the burp was the smile that spread across DJ's face. "Maybe she is a Farraday."

"Don't let your aunt hear you say that. According to her, Farradays have only honorable genes."

"True." More comfortable with the baby, DJ stepped toward the living room, still patting little Brittany. "If you can get me some sheets, I'll set up my bed."

"About that." Becky handed him the bottle, and waited for him to shift Brittany into the crook of his arm so he could feed her the remainder of the bottle contents. When he seemed settled into the concept and not likely to keel over from nerves, she continued, "There's no way you'll get anything close to sleep folded onto my sofa. You take the bedroom and I'll sleep out here."

"Not happening," he whispered.

"I won't sleep a wink worrying about you squeezing six foot three—"

"Four."

"Okay, squeezing six foot four worth of police chief onto a five foot sofa. I, on the other hand, will fit just fine."

Staring at the baby, he shook his head. "She's not drinking any more. I think she's sleeping."

Becky moved closer, eased the nearly empty bottle away from the baby and held it up. "She's got a good appetite." Before she could tell him it was time to burp her again, DJ had Brittany on his shoulder and was patting her back.

"Now what?" he asked.

"You put her down in the crib and hope we all get some sleep before the next round."

"Where are the sheets?" he asked.

"Take the bed."

"I can't."

"Of course you can. I just happened to have changed the sheets this morning."

"That's not what I meant." DJ chuckled.

"Please." Becky turned back the covers.

DJ shook his head. "Trust me when I tell you I've slept soundly in more cramped places than your living room sofa."

She'd forgotten that DJ had spent his share of time in the marines too and didn't like the mental images that single sentence brought to mind. All the more reason she needed to figure out a way for him to take her room. "I could always hang a blanket down the middle of the bed."

"The walls of Jericho." DJ smiled again. "Great movie. But I'm not sure who would come at me with a butcher knife first, your grandmother or my aunt."

"They can't object to sleeping."

DJ's brows arched high on his forehead. "Are we talking about the same women?"

"Yeah, I am. Come on. It's just a place to sleep."

Easing Brittany out of his arms and onto the crib. DJ shook his head, and tiptoeing out of the room, mumbled something suspiciously like, "Famous last words."

CHAPTER SIX

"What could be so all fired important to drag me out of bed two mornings in a row?" Sally May Henderson shrugged out of her windbreaker by the back table of the Silver Spoon Café.

Eileen Callahan, the Farraday brothers' aunt, was already dealing the cards.

"For land sakes, can't a gal have a minute to even order a cup of coffee?" Sally May dropped into the only empty seat and hurriedly gathered her cards.

"Ante up," Eileen said, neatly stacking the deck beside her.

"I know. I know." Sally May grabbed a white chip and tossed into the center of the table. "You'd think we were playing for real money."

Dorothy pulled two cards from her hand, set them face down on the table, and then looked over to Eileen. "I'm in. Two cards." She quickly sorted the new playing cards into her hand, fanned them closed, set them on the table and waited as the bets came around the table back to her. "I'll see your five, Ruth Ann, and raise you five more."

"I'm out." Ruth Ann tossed in her hand.

"Me too." Sally May folded.

Eileen eyed her friend carefully, fanned her cards open and closed, and then dropping a couple of chips into the pot, leaned forward, facing Dorothy. "It can't be what you're thinking."

Sally May eyed the two longtime friends. This was something new. For years, the Saturday morning card games and occasional weekday games had been lighthearted rivalry with a little good-natured ribbing and a healthy dose of community gossip. Even the time that Adam had driven into town at the crack of dawn with a beautiful stranger, no one's nose got bent out of joint. This little tête-à-tête looked a tad too serious.

Leaning forward, Ruth Ann shifted her attention from Dorothy to Eileen and back. "Are either of you two going to clue the rest of us in on what the heck is going on?"

Laying all her cards open faced on the table—a straight, ace high—Dorothy crossed her arms. "Maybe we should start by asking whose car was parked in front of the vet clinic at the crack of dawn."

"He's a police officer." Eileen stared at her friend. "DJ could have been parked there for a million different reasons."

Ruth Ann's eyes opened wide and Sally May was pretty sure hers were bulging with surprise too. "DJ spent the night with Becky?"

In a synchronized movement, Dorothy and Eileen's heads snapped around to face Ruth Ann, only one voice declared "no," while the other insisted, "yes."

Sally May shook her head. "Do you mean to tell me you dragged me out of a peaceful slumber and had me drive all the way down here because two of our town's citizens are making a little whoopie?"

This time Dorothy and Eileen's heads spun around to face Sally May, and she had a dang good understanding of where the expression "If looks could kill" came from.

"Okay." Ruth Ann held up her hands. "Ignoring that we have two red-blooded American adults perfectly within their rights to get... friendly, if they so choose," Ruth sucked in a breath, "let's assume for a minute it's not what we're all thinking."

"Thank you," Eileen said, setting her cards face up. Queens over aces. "I believe that trumps your straight."

"This isn't bridge." Dorothy scooped up her cards.

"No," Eileen agreed, "and there has to be a good reason for DJ spending the night at Becky's."

"How do we know he spent the night?" Sally May dared to ask. "All you said is he was there early in the morning. Could there have been an animal emergency that he needed to bring in? Someone's pet hit by a car, something like that?"

Eileen shook her head. "I phoned an order into the hardware store this morning for Finn. Burt didn't waste any time telling me how nice it is that one of my boys had noticed what a great catch Becky is. I told him we've all been saying that for years—"

"Damn straight," Dorothy interjected.

"Then he added he just hadn't thought it would be DJ. Next he told me how he'd seen DJ heading up the apartment stairs last night after dark and noticed the patrol car still there this morning."

"Okay. But that doesn't mean—" Sally May started.

"No, it doesn't," Eileen directed at Dorothy. "Besides, everyone knows Becky only has eyes for Ethan. There just has to be another reason."

"There is." Dorothy leaned forward, her mouth open ready to spit fire when she sat back unexpectedly, her shoulders sagging, and blew out a deep breath. "You're right. My Becky's not stupid and DJ's as honorable as they come. I guess I'm just afraid of what could be wrong in my grandbaby's life that she needs police protection all night."

Sally May gathered the rest of the cards into a pile and began shuffling. "Well, at least we know she hasn't been left at the altar or threatened by an almost ex-husband."

"No." Ruth Ann cut the deck. "There is that."

"Have you just asked DJ what's going on?" Sally May dealt a new round of cards.

"No." Eileen scooped up the first card. "I don't like to butt into my boys' personal lives."

Blinking long and hard so as not to roll her eyes or laugh out right in her friend's face, Sally May quickly turned to Dorothy. "Have you asked Becky?"

The devoted grandmother shrugged a shoulder and shook her head. "Which is why we invited Meg and Toni to join us."

Sally May looked to Ruth Ann who both rolled her eyes and shrugged. Why go straight to the horse's mouth when you can drag in all the relatives instead. She'd give her friends credit for one thing: when you want to get to the root of the matter, no one liked to gossip more than in-laws. "Are they coming?"

Dorothy shrugged again. "Not till lunchtime. Toni's baking and Meg has guests."

"Which is why," Eileen folded her hand and leaned into the table, lowering her voice, "we're here so early." The woman looked left then right and smiling continued, "Esther has been on dispatch for the last two days."

A collective "ah" sounded. Bobbing her head with approval, Dorothy smiled at her friend. "And she's on today too."

Eileen nodded and leaned back. "Yep." Spreading her cards in her hand again, she looked over the top at Dorothy. "Should be here any—" The old-fashioned overdoor bell jingled, making Eileen's smile broaden. "—minute."

Apparently, Dorothy and Eileen's backup plans had backups. Per Esther's usual routine when she came into the café for her morning coffee break, she ordered a tall coffee black and a slice of Frank's pie of the day. Occasionally she'd go for a few of Toni's cakeballs, but mostly she stuck with pie. Sometimes a la mode. And if there was a card game going on, she always pulled up a chair to visit with the social club. Hence the impromptu second game of the week.

This morning was no different. Esther raised her mirrored sunglasses onto her head, and resting one hand on her utility belt, scanned the café. Her gaze landing on the table of card playing women, her face softened with a smile as she made her way to the table, nodding and exchanging a few words with patrons as she passed. "Weren't you ladies just playing cards yesterday?"

Ruth Ann cast a furtive glance in Eileen's direction, but the woman was a pro at subterfuge. No doubt she had a brilliant excuse at the ready. She probably would have made a fantastic military spy.

"Mornin', Esther." Eileen waved. "Seemed like a nice morning to spend with friends."

Sally May blinked. *That* was all Eileen could come up with?

"Any day is a good day for friends." Somewhere around middle age, give or take a decade, a slender woman with hair pulled back into a tight bun, Esther straddled the line between a prima ballerina and lady's prison warden. She leaned over Ruth Ann's shoulder, and when Ruth touched a card, Esther shook her head.

"You should join us on your days off," Dorothy suggested, setting down a card. "No money, no gambling, no laws broken."

"I know." The police officer nodded at Ruth Ann's second choice and leaned back so Abbie could set her order on the table. "Just doesn't look right to have an off-duty police officer at a poker table."

Without moving their heads, the social club ladies glanced back and forth at each other. None of them understood how sitting at a poker table in full uniform—even just to observe—was less problematic than playing cards on a Saturday morning in civilian clothes.

Dorothy dealt the new cards. Sally May suspected everyone stayed in the game more for something to do than because they had a potentially winning hand.

"I hear you've been pretty busy at the station house." Eileen picked up her card without looking at Esther, knowing full well those were the only words she'd need for a river of information to pour out.

"Yep." Esther took a sip and showed no sign of saying anything more.

Hand frozen over her cards, Eileen looked up. If Esther was keeping quiet, something more important than mailbox bashing was going on.

"Heard from Burt Larson that one of the Brady boys has a broken arm?"

"That's what I hear." Esther seemed more relaxed.

Eileen moved her cards around in her hand. "Sounds like DJ's got his Louisville Slugger."

"Could be. Never know." Esther was being suspiciously close mouthed.

"I'm out." Ruth Ann tossed her cards down. "Poor DJ has to be awfully busy with the mailboxes and...all."

"Mm."

"Oh for heaven's sake." Eileen laid her cards down on the table. "What happened yesterday out of the ordinary?"

"Not much." Esther picked up her fork, stabbed at her pie. Her hand midway to her mouth, she stopped and looked at Eileen. "Unless you're talking about the baby."

CHAPTER SEVEN

Swallowing the last drop of coffee he'd picked up at the café, DJ turned into the Brady driveway. The original Brady ranch had been divvied up amongst the children when their grandfather passed on twenty or more years ago. As each grandchild married, they received a good size parcel. Jim and his wife had turned to raising sheep and now had added alpacas to the mix. Apparently, the wool business did well for them. Jim's wife stayed home and none of the kids ever seemed to lack love or the basics. They drove nice enough vehicles and the house was pretty and well maintained. With eight children, much like his parents, they were a throwback to the American family at the turn of the century—the last century. He hated to be the one to put a crack in the perfect picture frame.

"DJ." Mary Brady had spotted him coming up the drive and like a good country hostess, stood ready to greet him at the door. "Isn't this a nice surprise. You needing another donation for the town fundraiser?"

DJ waited till he was in front of her to slip his sunglasses into his pocket and remove his hat. "'Fraid not."

"Oh." Her smile slipped just a pinch.

"Is Christopher around?"

Color drained from her face and she nodded her head. "He broke his arm horsing around with some friends. Doc said he should take it easy for a couple of days. 'Course that's easier said than done. You know how boys are. Always full of energy." She waved him into the house.

He smiled and offered a polite nod. "I'd like to ask him a few questions."

"Of course. Follow me."

Inside the large den, the twins were corralled in an oversize playpen. One on his feet, gnawing on the padded edges, the other sitting in the middle happily stacking miscellaneous-shaped building blocks. So alike and so different. On the sofa, DJ's prime suspect was surrounded with food, drink, and a stack of videos that told DJ the kid was getting the royal worried mother treatment. Well, that would be changing shortly.

"Christopher, Police Chief Farraday's here to talk to you."

DJ almost laughed at the stricken look that crossed the kid's face. *Busted.*

There hadn't been any need for an inquisition. The kid stiffened his upper lip, lifted his chin, and too quickly said, "It wasn't me."

Hands on her hips, Mary Brady's gaze narrowed on her middle son. "What wasn't you?"

And that was that. The kid spilled his guts, and by the time his mother was finished with him, he was pretty much grounded for life, and all DJ had asked was, "How's the arm?"

DJ suspected that this was either going to be the end or the beginning. By the time Jim Brady made his way back to the house and reminded his son of what was expected from him, the kid had given up the names of his cohorts, agreed to rebuild each and every mailbox, as well as do extra chores at the five homes. And pretty much anything else the homeowners ask of him, for what might prove to be the rest of his underage life. Christopher would either straighten up or if there was a next time, find his way to the inside of a cell.

For the kid's sake DJ hoped it never came to the latter. Now, back in his office, he downed another cup of coffee, not sure if he would ever be truly awake again. What he didn't get was after parents spent months of sleepless nights with one child, why would they have any more? And his parents had had seven. He shook his head and took another sip.

"What you need is a nap." Esther stood in the doorway, a covered dish in hand. "I brought you a piece of Frank's blueberry pie. You'll get a nice sugar rush."

"Until I crash."

"If you're gonna keep helping the Wilson girl take care of that baby, you'd better get used to sugar rushes. That may be all that keeps you going until they find the parents or the baby graduates high school."

High school? That had DJ looking up.

"What? You think a parent's problems stop when the baby sleeps through the night? Lord, no. There's colic." She stopped halfway to his desk. "Does the baby have colic?"

He thought what colic meant with the ranch animals. "Don't think so."

"How often is she waking up?" Esther set the dish in front of him.

"Every. Two. Hours."

A knowing grin slid across his dispatcher's face. "Gotta love babies." She sighed. "Like I was saying, after they get to sleeping through the night, then there's teething, and walking, and terrible twos, trying threes." Esther stopped and shook her head. "But all you have to last through is a few nights till they find the parents or a permanent home for that little one." She waved a finger at the dish on his desk. "Better eat up. You're gonna need all the energy you can get."

Several things crossed DJ's mind. First was a newfound respect for single parents everywhere. He understood he was supposed to be staying at Becky's to help. The delusion being that by taking turns they would get more sleep. In fact, all that happened was one would rock or change the diaper while the other heated the bottle. And if by some chance one of them, usually Becky, managed to change, feed, *and* rock the baby back to sleep on their own, the other one of them was wide awake and alert in case they were needed. He definitely needed to give single parents way more credit.

Following Brooklyn's instructions for a quick DNA analysis, the infant's swab was sealed and bagged and ready to send off for evaluation. Finn hadn't found anything at the ranch of Ethan's that could easily be used for DNA testing. Though they'd discussed a pair of riding gloves, the chances of making that work were too low. Instead DJ did a swab of his own and figured mitochondrial DNA would at least pinpoint if Brittany was a Farraday. Unless another brother indulged in a little R&R at the marine air base—unlikely with none of the brothers leaving town for more than a few hours in over a year—the only way Brittany's dad could share DNA with D.J. would be if Ethan was indeed the proud papa. So both samples were now ready for the hour of truth.

Which brought DJ back to other thoughts knocking around in his brain. If indeed this sweet baby, and she certainly was sweet, proved to be Ethan's daughter, there was no way in hell Ethan could care for her. Not only was his deployment a problem, but Ethan's swashbuckling nature did not blend well with burping a baby all night long. Which meant, at least for now, someone else would have to care for her. The logical choice would be Aunt Eileen. She certainly knew more about raising little girls than any of his brothers. Probably knew more about it than his dad too. His sister Grace turned out all right, even if she was a bit on the free-spirited side. He didn't doubt his sister's strengths were all Aunt Eileen's doing. Lord only knows how she would have turned out with a bunch of boys bringing her up. Of course, any of his married or soon to be married brothers could take on the job. Not that raising your brother's baby was a great way to start a marriage.

Scrubbing at his face as though the gesture would be enough to wash away the exhaustion and frustration, he blew out a bellowing sigh and wondered how Becky was holding up with Brittany at work.

• • • •

"At this rate, we might as well stop pretending to get any work done." Kelly swayed with Brittany while Pat, the lab tech, stood nearby waiting her turn.

And that hadn't taken into account the time Becky had spent introducing her to all the clients in the waiting room, or feeding, changing, and rocking her.

"How's our girl doing?" Adam came in from the large animal building out back. He'd just finished doing a thorough horse checkup for a new family moving into town. One finger sticking straight out, Adam used it to tickle the baby's tummy.

So far, Brittany hadn't shared a smile, but instead did a great deal of studying the people around her. While she didn't seem abused or mistreated, no diaper rash or anything else that would indicate she'd been less than well cared for, there simply weren't any contented smiles.

"You're frowning, Becky." Adam straightened and took a step away from the baby. "Something wrong?"

"Oh nothing. Wool gathering again."

"Right." Adam smiled and shook his head. "Are we ordering lunch to eat here or taking the baby to the café?"

"Word's out," Pat said over her shoulder. "So it doesn't much matter what you do."

Of course, Nadine Peabody and her hussy cat Sadie had been the first patient this morning. The woman was second in line to Burt Larson as the best gossip in town. She had barely set foot out the door before neighbors and friends began phoning or popping by to check on the little girl.

"I'm pretty sure there's a pool going too." Kelly handed the infant off to Pat. "According to Ned from the garage, with those pretty blue eyes, odds are really low on the brown-eyed bachelors in town, but if her eyes start to change any time soon..." Kelly wiggled her brows and laughed.

The betting pool gave them all something to joke about, but there wasn't anything very funny about it for Becky. Deep down in her gut she felt sure the mother hadn't lied on the birth certificate and this little girl was a Farraday. And if the way Brittany studied everyone who came near was any indication, she would grow up to be a smart Farraday. Maybe even a military pilot like her daddy. "They don't let stupid people fly planes," she mumbled.

"What?" Baby on her shoulder, Pat spun around to face Becky.

"Just muttering to myself."

"About what?" Pat asked again.

"We're spoiling her." Becky sure didn't want to repeat what she'd been thinking. "She hasn't been put down for five minutes since we got here this morning. I'm just wondering which one of you is going to be pacing the floors with her when three in the morning rolls around."

"Did I hear the phone ring?" Pat handed back the baby with a final gentle pat.

"I guess I should get at least a little bit of work done." Kelly retreated a step, still close enough to gently rub her hand along the baby's downy soft hair, and at the same time keep an eye on Adam as he closed his office door behind him. "But if it means warming up to DJ Farraday, I might be willing to volunteer for a little late night visit." Her voice had intentionally dropped an octave to give the statement a Mae West affect.

It worked. The old catch phrase, *Why don't you come up and see me some time*, shot instantly to mind and Becky was none too pleased about it. Not that she had any interest or claim in DJ, but...*but what?*

"You're frowning again." Kelly looked up at her friend.

No buts. She didn't like Kelly teasing about DJ and she didn't need a reason to not like it. "I thought you had some spreadsheets to get to."

"So much like your grandmother," Kelly mumbled on her way back to the front desk.

Growing up, Becky had hated being compared to her mother or grandmother. Two bossy women. By the time she was out of high school, it struck her that the women in her family were strong, kind, dependable *and* respected and loved by everyone around them. Including by her. Being compared to her grandmother now was just about the best compliment she could get.

With Brittany asleep on her shoulder, Becky reluctantly eased the infant onto the cradle pad in the break room and resisted the temptation to lay down beside her and catch a few winks of her own. Now would be a good time to check in with Grace.

Sitting down at the nearby computer, she pulled up the messaging program and hit chat. Blinking a few times, she'd almost closed the program and lay her head on the desk when a ding had her springing upright.

Bright smile and all, Grace appeared on the screen. "Well, hi stranger."

It had been quite a few days since they'd spoken. "Pot calling kettle black. I'm not the one up to my eyeballs in textbooks."

"Ugh," Grace groaned. "Don't remind me. Have I mentioned how much I hate tests?"

Becky laughed. "Since pre-school."

"We didn't have tests in pre-school." Grace rolled her eyes. "Remind me again why I thought law school was a good idea."

"Seriously? You're asking me that now?"

This time Grace was the one to offer a muffled laugh. "Okay, so I'm just whining a little. What has you online in the middle of work day?"

"A baby."

Grace's eyes circled wide and her face took up the whole screen as she leaned forward. "You're pregnant?"

"No. You have to have sex to get pregnant."

"Okay," Grace eased back in her chair. "You had me there for a minute. So why *are* you online?"

"There really is a baby. I'm the temporary foster parent."

"Ah." Grace bobbed her head. "Now it all makes sense. And explains the rings under the eyes. You look like hell."

"Gee, thanks." Obviously none of the brothers had contacted Grace to update her on what was going on, and Becky didn't feel comfortable spilling all the beans. "She was left on the police station steps."

Scowling, Grace sprang forward again. "In Tuckers Bluff? Do we know who the worthless mother is?"

Becky shook her head. "Only a name. She's not from here."

"How do you know her name?"

"She left a birth certificate and release of parental rights."

"Sounds pretty tidy." A rap on the door sounded and Grace looked down to the corner of the screen. "Crap, I'm late. Have to run. Tell big brother to shoot me a copy of the papers and I'll take a look at them. See if they're on the up and up."

"Will do." Becky waved at the computer. Grace waved back and then the screen went black.

Rubbing her eyes, Becky blew out a sigh, her forehead resting on the heels of her palm.

"I know how you feel." DJ's voice carried from the doorway. He'd spoken softly, but the deep timbre carried easily. "I gather she's behaving."

Becky nodded. "Hard not to with all the attention she's getting."

"You'd think she was the Second Coming the way word is spreading around town." He stepped closer to watch the sleeping baby.

"Everyone loves a good mystery. Whose baby is she? Why was she left in Tuckers Bluff? Is the mama local or the daddy or both? Lots of questions. Same ones Grace asked."

"You spoke?"

Becky nodded. "Just for a few minutes. She was running late. I told her about the baby but not about Ethan."

"What did she say?"

"For you to send her the papers the mother left and she'd see if they were on the up and up."

One side of his mouth tipped up with amusement. He was most likely thinking the same thing she was. Sometimes it was hard to picture free-spirited Grace as a by-the-book-lawyer.

"I don't know what I would have said if she'd asked too many questions."

DJ looked from the baby to Becky. "I sent the samples overnight. We'll have some information soon."

Becky wasn't sure how she felt about that. A huge part of her liked the idea of Ethan having a reason to come home and stay home. Another part of her wondered if he would simply take Brittany away closer to his base. Or maybe track down the mother and marry her. Of all the options, the latter made the most sense. The Farradays were fiercely loyal. Proud and honorable rolled easily off anyone's tongue when talking about the family. As old fashioned as it sounded, doing the right thing would be exactly that for a Farraday. Even Ethan. Then there was always the remote possibility that the mother had lied. Had simply put the name of the nicest guy she'd slept with on the birth certificate and hoped for the best. Becky wished she knew more about the woman.

"I notified social services." DJ lowered his voice even further, as though afraid the baby might hear and be offended. "As expected, they're swamped, but we can expect a visit from the county in the not too distant future."

"How soon do you think?"

DJ shrugged. "Could be tomorrow as easily as it could be next month. I'm hoping whenever the county sees fit to get heavily involved, it's after we know if she's a Farraday."

"What about the mother? Will they need to contact her?"

Shaking his head, DJ ran a hand behind his neck and looked up. "The last envelope contained a voluntary termination of parental rights."

"Boy," Becky turned her attention to the sleeping baby, "she really doesn't want her daughter, does she?"

"I think that was pretty clear when she left Brittany in a box alone on a doorstep," DJ snapped.

Becky sucked in a breath. She wasn't used to snarky responses from him or his brothers. All the years she'd spent hanging out with Grace at the Farraday house, and as often as she and Grace harassed or pranked them, not once had they barked at her.

"Sorry." DJ blew out a heavy sigh. "I'm a little tired."

"I was just thinking about the time Grace and I painted Adam's toenails while he was sleeping."

One side of DJ's mouth tipped upward.

"When he woke up and realized his toenails—and most of his toes—were shocking pink, he went after you and Connor."

"I remember," DJ said. "He had me pinned against the wall by the collar when you two came into the room and Grace asked if he didn't like the color."

"That's when I said, *I told you to use red.*" Becky couldn't stop from smiling. Her memories of growing up with the Farradays felt like home. "Adam looked at us with our fingers and toes painted red and pink, then letting go of your shirt took a step toward us, squatted, and very calmly for a sixteen-year-old said, *please don't do that again without asking.*"

DJ shrugged. "Adam always tried to be the reasonable one."

"So did you." She wondered if he'd remember what she was thinking about.

His eyes narrowed a moment before recollection hit. "Ah. The eye shadow." The other side of his mouth tilted up to even out his smile. "You were older then. Six, I think."

Becky nodded. "When you woke up—"

"Because Adam and Brooks were laughing so hard," he added.

"Yes. You didn't get angry, you let us put blush and lipstick on you too."

"It made sense. You both were having fun and it wasn't like Adam or Brooks could laugh any harder." He chuckled and shook his head. "And thank God there were no cell phone cameras in those days."

"True."

"I'm sorry I snapped. With everything else going on, this situation is fraying on my last nerve."

"Anything I can help with?"

He glanced at the baby and up at her. "You already are." His cell sounded. "Farraday."

Becky couldn't hear who was on the other end.

DJ squeezed his eyes, mumbled *shit* and turned on his heel. "Have Reed meet me and then call Brooks. I'll be there in a minute."

The way DJ had already crossed the office at a brisk pace, Becky knew whatever was happening, it wasn't good. "Be careful."

DJ spun around to face her. She had the distinct feeling he'd forgotten she was in the room. He nodded and tore through the waiting room and out the door.

"Where's the fire?" Kelly asked.

Becky shrugged.

"Oh my God." Pat came running from the back. "Polly from the Cut and Curl just called. Jake Thomas has gone berserk. He's locked himself in the feed store." Pat sucked in a deep breath, scanning the area. "Where's Doc?"

"Exam room 2." Kelly waved a thumb over her shoulder.

"I need to tell him about Meg."

Adam opened the exam room door in time to catch Pat's words. "What about my wife?"

"Jake Thomas has locked himself in the feed store with Charlotte and Meg."

"Damn it." Turning quickly, he tossed the chart in his hand onto the counter as he passed. "Reschedule everyone."

He was already halfway to the door, when Pat called after him, "Doc. He has a gun."

CHAPTER EIGHT

In a town this small, there was little need to run the patrol car with lights and sirens, especially if he didn't want half the town following him the few blocks, but damn if right about now, DJ didn't wish he could fly.

From the other direction, Reed's car squealed into an empty space in front of the feed store. He was out of the car and positioned at the far edge of the brick building by the time DJ had reached the storefront. Taking only an extra minute, he circled around to the trunk, pulled out his vest and drew in a deep breath. He thought he'd never have to use one of these again. Grabbing the nearby rifle, he sucked in more air. With any luck, the only thing in his sights today would be at the other end of the binoculars now hanging around his neck. Trotting the long way around out of Jake's line of vision, DJ came to a stop by his junior officer. "What have we got?"

Reed shook his head. "I can only see Jake. He seems to be pacing at the back of the store. Hasn't looked up. I don't think he knows we're here."

"Who called it in?"

"I did." Ned came hurrying over from his garage. "We were just jawing about the weather and how maybe this summer won't be a scorcher."

DJ nodded and hoped for the abridged version.

"Meg Farraday came in, seems she and Charlotte were going to lunch. Or was it shopping?"

"Doesn't matter. What happened?" DJ prompted.

"That's just it. I don't know." He shrugged. "I said something about how pretty the ladies looked and Jake exploded. The phone rang and he yanked the cord out of the wall. I knew something wasn't right, especially when I saw the way his wife flinched and Meg shifted to stand in front of her."

"Meg stood in front of Charlotte?"

Ned nodded. "Like she was going to protect her or something. I may be too old to put up a good fight, but I can still think. I shook my head, smiled and said, 'some days I'd like to do just that to my old phone.' I'd hoped it would put him at ease, but it just seemed to fire him up. He looked like that TV character who turned green."

Ned went quiet and Reed provided, "The Hulk."

"Yeah," Ned nodded again. "That one. Before I could say another word Jake pulled that old handgun out of the drawer and waved it around. Meg and Charlotte dived for the floor and I went for the gun."

If what the old man said was true, DJ hoped the fact Ned was still standing in one piece and not sprawled along the feed store floor in small bits meant no one would be carried out in a body bag today.

"He fired into the ceiling."

"On purpose?" DJ asked.

"Sure looked like it. He yelled for everyone to get out. I waited for the girls by the door. Next thing I knew Jake shoved me outside and pushed them back before locking the door behind me. Didn't have no cell phone. Ran back to the shop and called you."

As if on cue Polly from the Cut and Curl came running over. Just what DJ needed, the whole town popping by for a visit.

"I called as soon as I heard the gun shot. Didn't want to believe that's what it was, but I could see Jake waving that thing around."

DJ looked from the feed store to the Cut and Curl all the way across Main Street. "You saw him?"

The petite woman blushed and blinked. "I may have been using the binoculars we keep under the register."

When DJ had more time, he'd give that tidbit of information some thought. "What else did you see?"

"Jake moved Meg and Charlotte to the back wall. They're on the floor huddled side by side. Jake's been pacing ever since."

"Did you hear anything he said?"

Polly straightened and frowned. "I said binoculars, not microphone. What kind of a neighbor do you think I am?"

Another question for another day. "Okay, thanks. You go on back to your shop and stay indoors."

She nibbled on her lower lip and shook her head. "Never thought I'd see anything like this in my lifetime. Not in Tuckers Bluff."

Neither the hell had he. Just then Adam's truck came barreling down the street.

"Reed, radio Esther. I want you and her to barricade the street. No one else, except Brooks, comes anywhere near here. You got that?"

Reed barely gave a nod, before setting off at a trot.

"Is she okay?" The big quad cab had barely come to a stop when Adam tumbled out of it and rushed at DJ.

"Hold on there." DJ stuck his arm straight out. "Take a deep breath. They're fine." He wasn't going to say *so far* out loud.

"Is it true? Does Jake have a gun on them?" Adam was a strong man. As strong as they came, but the worry in his eyes seemed enough to break him.

"We haven't confirmed it, but it seems likely." DJ nudged his brother aside. "I know this is hard, but I need you to stay out of the way. This isn't like last time."

"No." Adam frowned at his brother's reference to Meg and her ex. "This time Meg doesn't have a secret weapon."

"That we know of. She's a smart woman. Trust her." DJ shifted his weight. "And me."

Staring at him a little longer, Adam let his gaze lift to the large feed store window and then slowly settle back on DJ. "Don't let anything happen to her."

All DJ could do was nod. Losing anyone wasn't on his agenda for the day.

• • • •

The old saying "Telegraph, telephone, and tell-a-woman" apparently was alive and well and living in West Texas. Word of Jake going postal was spreading through Tuckers Bluff like fire in a hayfield. According to snowballing gossip, the hostages ranged from a few to dozens and the weapons varied from a single police issue handgun to an arsenal of rapid-fire assault weapons and anything and everything in between.

The only thing Becky knew for sure to be true was that Meg and Charlotte were inside the feed store and things had to be pretty damn serious for all the surrounding shops along Main Street to be evacuated. For as long as Becky could remember, two officers and a dispatcher always worked the day shifts and one officer worked the quiet graveyard shift alone. Knowing that at least one of the off duty officers had been called in to help made this whole thing feel like a TV crime show, not real life in Tuckers Bluff.

The surreal situation probably explained why most of the displaced shopkeepers and other neighbors had found their way to the Silver Spurs.

Without Adam to tend to the patients the clinic had shut down early. No one could concentrate on work and eventually they'd all come to the café to wait the crisis out as well, even Becky.

"How long has it been?" Kelly asked, stirring a teaspoon of sugar into another cup of coffee.

"Almost an hour and if you don't stop chugging that liquid caffeine, we're going to be peeling you off the ceiling long before this is over." Abbie waved a finger at the full coffee mug.

Pacing with the baby, Becky had been able to keep her nerves at bay. Sort of. The truth was, she was worried sick about everyone. The image of Adam's stricken face as he literally ran out of the clinic tore at her heart. She didn't want to think what Meg and Charlotte must be going through, held hostage by a crazy man, or what that crazy man might do to them and the police gathered outside.

Last night, she'd seen a new side to DJ. Another dimension to a man she'd thought rather serious. Words like sweet and tender came to mind and she didn't like how those fit with bullets flying. For almost an hour, DJ had been dialoging with Jake Thomas. Word on the street was that the state police had been called in and any minute now the town would be swarming with all sorts of police and federal agencies. Others insisted DJ had been some kind of super-SWAT-special-forces-star-spangled-cop and didn't need anyone's help to talk Jake out of the mess he'd gotten himself into. Truthfully, Becky had no idea where reality came into play. She'd followed Ethan's career, not DJ's, but hoped to God that star-spangled-super-cop was the first line on his resume.

"Do you think it's true?" Pat asked, her gaze trained down the road to the police barricade.

"What?" Becky said.

"That DJ has done this before?"

Kelly shook her head. "All Grace ever said about Dallas was that he'd made detective. I'd think if he'd been in hostage negotiations she would have said something. I mean, that sounds sort of cool to a baby sister."

"From where I stand, it sounds pretty damn frightening." Abbie exchanged the mostly full water glasses on the table for fresh ones. No one in the place was eating and Becky suspected the café owner needed to keep herself busy.

"I wouldn't be surprised if he was." The words were out of Becky's mouth before she'd given them much thought. She remembered back when DJ had made Detective in Dallas, that Grace had bragged he'd moved up the ranks pretty damn fast. Becky also remembered something being said about opportunities coming more easily for former military. Another time, she'd overheard snippets of a conversation between her boss and his brother. She wasn't sure if DJ had been talking in generalities or if he'd been having a problem of his own, but he'd said that lots of good men resented the crap out of being passed over for the coveted detective spots. The words had never been said, but she'd gotten the impression that whatever DJ had done in the marines had more than qualified him for whatever promotions the Dallas police department doled out. "I think he can do it."

"I know he can," Abbie mumbled softly.

The bell over the front door jingled and all heads turned to see Sean Farraday stride inside with the youngest Farraday son and Aunt Eileen at his side. "I don't know what you expected," the older woman said.

"He's not doing anyone any good pacing like a panther on the prowl." Sean hung his hat on the nearest hook and glanced about until his gaze landed on Abbie. "DJ wants some sandwiches for Jake and the girls."

"Coming right up." Abbie turned toward the kitchen. "One order—"

"I heard," Frank shouted from the kitchen, "though it chafes my butt to give that ass...man anything." His gruff voice dropped as he continued to mumble, "If DJ thinks a sandwich will put Jake back in his right mind, I'll slice and butter every loaf of bread in Tuckers Bluff."

Eileen put a hand on Sean Farraday's forearm. "See if you can't get Adam to eat a little something too. This could be a very long day."

Staring a long while at his sister-in-law, the patriarch of the Farraday clan barely nodded before Eileen spotted Becky and headed straight for her.

"So this is the mystery baby?" Softly patting her hands in front of Brittany, Aunt Eileen smiled and cooed in complete contrast to her grave conversation of moments ago.

Becky had to wonder what the woman would do if she knew who Brittany's daddy was. Or might be.

CHAPTER NINE

"You still doing okay in there?" DJ asked again. His mouth had run dry from talking.

"Why do you care?" The recent sadness in Jake's voice indicated the situation had shifted. The rash anger that had filled the man's earlier responses was gone. Jake seemed on a slow train back to sanity.

Unable to see the happenings inside since Jake lowered the shades on the glass doors, DJ had to determine everything from Jake's tone. And right about now, he sounded more tired than anything else. "Just want to help. It's been a long day. You must be tired."

"Of course I'm tired," Jake snapped. "Can't you leave us alone?" Something had shifted and not for the better.

DJ had heard the sound of desperation teetering on exhaustion before when reality began to set in. He needed to shift gears. A new approach. "You love your wife, don't you?"

"Of course I do." The weariness was back.

Good. DJ could work with tired. Desperate was a whole hell of a lot more dangerous.

"Charlotte's the best thing that ever happened to me," Jake added.

"I'm thinking she feels the same way about you?" Lord knows neither he nor Brooks could convince her to leave Jake, not even for her own safety.

"Yeah, she loved me."

Jake's use of past tense sounded another alarm. Damn. Had he shifted the conversation in the wrong direction? DJ was too close to this. Meg was like a sister. Losing her would destroy Adam. *Damn it, no*. He couldn't afford to let his mind go there. Couldn't second-guess himself. He had no choice but to follow his instincts. "I've never had anyone to love. My brothers have. Adam loves Meg the way you love Charlotte." He sucked in a breath and waited, willing a positive response. Another beat of silence passed and DJ shifted in place, coming alert like a pedigree on point when the front door creaked open a crack.

Poised at either side of the building, Reed and Esther drew their guns and DJ held them off, praying neither had an itchy trigger finger.

The door inched open further and the wind carried voices in his direction. A voice. Meg's voice. "Please," she said once, then twice.

This time DJ moved forward a step, his hand on the butt of his gun, his heart rate kicking up a notch. Any wrong move could cost Meg her life.

"Don't make me—" Gunfire muffled Meg's cry as she flew from the open doorway, landing hard on the concrete.

The door slammed shut behind her and from the corner of his eye, DJ could see Reed holding Adam back. Bolting forward, placing himself between Meg and the door, DJ came to a crouch beside his sister-in-law, scanning for blood. "Are you okay?"

Already pushing to her feet, Meg pulled away. "Charlotte—"

Grabbing hold of her arm and practically lifting her off the sidewalk, he raced to where Brooks and Adam hovered at the edge of the building. "Are you hit?" He was pretty sure Jake had fired into the air again, but he had to make sure.

Shaking her head, she blinked back tears. "No. I'm fine."

Time was running out. He knew it as sure as he knew his name was Declan James Farraday.

Adam broke past Reed and nearly scooped his wife off the ground and into his arms.

DJ tapped her shoulder. "Meg, I'm sorry, but I need some answers. Now."

She pulled away from Adam and shooed away Brooks, who'd grabbed her wrist and starting playing doctor. "Oh, God, DJ. He's crazy. I've never seen anyone go so totally ballistic in my life. Not even…"

"It's okay. How many guns does he have?"

"I think just the one."

"You think."

She nodded. "Just the one."

"How many bullets has he fired?"

"One in the ceiling when he chased Ned out and one just now."

"Can you tell me anything at all he might have said about what he wants?"

Her head turned from side to side. "I don't understand. Perfectly normal one minute and then ranting and raving the next. Knocking over displays, throwing huge sacks of seed across the room as if they were lightweight balloons. It was like watching Superman."

Or the Hulk, he thought.

Gulping large breaths of air, Meg tightened her hold on her husband's hand. "Right after he told you Charlotte loved him, she told him she still did. Always would. God, how can anyone love a crazy man like that?"

Adam tucked his wife into his side and squeezing her shoulder, urged her to keep talking.

"He got quiet after that." She faced DJ. "Then you mentioned Adam and that's when Jake told us to get up. He apologized. Said he hadn't meant to scare me. It was like someone flipped a switch and Mr. Hyde was once again the docile Dr. Jekyll."

DJ looked over at Brooks. His brother nodded and DJ glanced to the shuttered door.

"I didn't want to leave her," Meg's voice cracked.

"You did good." He waved between Meg and Adam. "Both of you go home. You need some rest."

"No." Meg held her head high. Her stance straight. She stood immovable.

"Meg," Adam said softly.

"No. I'm not leaving here until Charlotte is safe."

Adam shrugged, Brooks lips pressed into a thin line and DJ, like his brothers, knew better than to insist. "Okay, but stay put. Reed doesn't need more work to do."

"Chief?" Reed shifted closer to his side. "Your father brought the food you asked for."

"Good."

Reed held out one of two bags. "Abbie sent root beer too. Says it's Jake's favorite."

"Perfect." DJ nodded.

"She also sent dessert. Told me to make sure and tell you Jake likes his root beer cold and his pie hot."

"That's my girl." Everything and anything to soothe the savage beast. Bless Abbie. Her extra contribution to the effort was almost enough to make DJ smile. Strong and smart—two words that described Abbie then and now. He knew too well that he could count on her to stay calm in a crisis.

Reed, the only other cop on the force who understood DJ's connection to Abbie, nodded.

Knowing Meg was in good hands and his officers had his back, DJ walked closer to the glass doors. Every little bit of normalcy now could only help. *Come on, answer.*

"What now?"

"I've got some food, Jake. Couple of bottles of root beer too."

"Root beer?" Jake's voice barely carried any strength.

"Two bottles."

Silence.

"They're nice and cold. Just put the gun down and I'll bring them in."

"No. You're trying to trick me."

"Not at all. Tell you what. Keep the gun, let Charlotte come out. I bet she's tired too. Probably wants to go home. Rest in her own bed."

"She stays with me. She promised."

"Okay. A wife should be by a man's side. I understand that. How about I put my gun down, then I'll bring in the food and drink and we can talk."

He heard Jake's voice low and quiet asking Charlotte if she was hungry. The depth of a woman's devotion to her abuser always seemed to surprise him. The phone must have been on speaker because Charlotte's response that he needed to eat too sounded through the phone loud and clear.

"Just my wife and me. Leave the food by the door. We'll be finished soon."

"Okay." DJ nodded at Reed and Esther. Each moved forward from their current positions. Lord how he wished to God that Jake was talking about the food, but he knew he'd just about run out of time. He placed the bags an arm's reach away from the door and repositioned himself where he'd been before. Taking in another deep breath, he drew his weapon and spoke into the phone. "Food's by the door. Root beer too. I've stepped away. It's all yours."

The next few seconds flew by in synchronized precision. Needing to open the door wider to reach the two bags, Jake stood in full view of DJ's sights. Jake's gun pointed where Adam and Meg had stood only moments ago. On DJ's cue, Esther yanked the door open wide, DJ moved in, Jake's arm spun around and DJ took his shot. Gun drawn, Reed rushed past him into the building. Adrenaline pumping, DJ kicked the gun away from the fallen man's hand and nodded at Brooks. Charlotte's piercing screams drowned out all other shouts of activity. God how he hated days like this.

• • • •

The sounds of a car backfiring ricocheted through the café. Except everyone in the place knew the blast had nothing to do with a car and everything to do with the situation at the feed store. The reverberations faded and every soul stared out the window, frozen in time, unable to see the bustle inside the barricades, waiting for the sound of more shots.

Nothing.

"That's a good thing. Right?" Becky's gaze remained fixed outside.

"Depends." Abbie's grip on the coffee pot tightened. "If an officer were down, we'd see all hell breaking loose. I'd say it's a safe guess our guys are secure."

Shortly after Sean Farraday left with food as DJ had requested, Connor and Catherine came in with little Stacey. Chatting and coloring, the little girl forced a lighter mood on all the patrons mulling about waiting. Until now.

At Becky's side, Aunt Eileen's shoulders deflated with relief and then equally fast, her eyes grew round as she spun about to face Abbie. "Meg?"

Abbie shook her head. "I honestly don't know, but if you're asking what I think, no more exchange of fire doesn't bode well for Jake. Either someone neutralized him…"

"Or he shot himself," Kelly said softly. "Poor Charlotte."

"I don't know about that, her life must be a living hell with that man." Aunt Eileen pointed up the street, her back straight again. "Looks like something's happening."

All eyes gravitated to the buzz of activity up Main Street. No one breathed a word until the lights of a Tuckers Bluff patrol car whipped down the street, the siren blaring, and Brooks' vehicle on its tail. What Abbie couldn't determine was if the injury was life threatening and the siren's whirring meant the cars were on their way to meet with a helicopter for transportation to Butler Springs, or if the injuries were minor enough that the long drive was an option.

Neither possibility sat well with Abbie.

"You okay?" Frank came up beside her as quietly as a Navy SEAL in the dead of night.

Abbie nodded. She'd been keeping busy. Busy helped block out the memories, keep the reminders at bay. "Better than I'd have thought."

Frank's gaze lingered from the top of her head to the tip of toes, carefully assessing his boss's state of mind. "That doesn't tell me much."

The concern in his gaze gave Abbie reason to smile. Lots of people cared about her here in Tuckers Bluff. People who mattered to her. "I'm okay. And you," she lifted her chin, pointing toward the kitchen, "need to get back to cooking. I'm expecting a very busy supper hour."

Frank took another second and then shrugging, turned his back to her, muttering, "Slave driver."

That made Abbie's smile widen. Tuckers Bluff was a good place to call home no matter what kind of madness just went down on Main Street.

CHAPTER TEN

"**M**ore tea?" Toni asked.

Becky shook her head. If she drank one more cup she'd float down Main Street. Her plans to go home with Brittany and wait for DJ had been discarded by Aunt Eileen hours ago.

Once the initial commotion after the stand-off had passed, Toni and Donna, one of the café waitresses, came into the Silver Spurs with Donna's baby girl. Toni had accompanied Donna to her doctor's appointment in Butler Springs to check out the obstetrician. Thank heaven Toni hadn't been in town during the most frightening moments. As it was, she'd blanched several shades of white while Aunt Eileen explained what had happened. No surprise to anyone, Meg had insisted on going with Charlotte to the hospital and of course Adam had insisted on going with Meg.

Once the conversation and activity at the café had returned to something close to normal, Connor and Stacey hitched a ride with Finn back to the ranch. There was only so much standing around men like that could do. Connor had been itching to get Stacey home in case any of the uniformed police came by, and Finn was just as happy to get back to his chores once he was sure everyone was perfectly safe and secure.

Sean Farraday, the rock that everyone leaned on, had only waited until everyone was accounted for and the blockades removed before taking his truck out to Butler Springs. Adam, Meg and Charlotte had driven with DJ in the patrol car. Sean was the only one to recognize that with Brooks and DJ both having jobs to do, Adam and Meg might need transportation home.

Having given Connor a goodbye kiss worthy of a Hollywood melodrama, Catherine stuck around for whenever Aunt Eileen needed a ride home. Based on her past losses, it was no surprise that she and Connor understood the value of loved ones more than anyone.

Since Aunt Eileen preferred to stay in town and wait for the remainder of her boys to come back from Butler Springs, the Farraday clan had moved to the B&B so Toni could tend to the few guests Meg had and wait for more news together. The way Aunt Eileen usually referred to her nephews as boys almost always gave Becky the giggles. Grown men, tall as trees, and they would always be Aunt Eileen's boys.

Conversation stilled at the rumble of a truck in the drive. It had been almost an hour since DJ had called from the hospital to let Becky know he was on his way back to town. One door slammed after another, then more engine sounds and more car doors slamming. Becky kept her gaze on the kitchen doorway of Adam and Meg's old Victorian bed and breakfast. With Meg tucked under his arm, Adam was the first in the door. DJ was next, followed by his father.

"Okay," Catherine looked at Meg, "I think it's time to put the tea pot away and break out the corkscrew. Red or white?"

"White," Meg answered without skipping a beat.

"Anyone else?" Catherine looked around the room.

"Make mine a scotch," Sean Farraday said from the other side of the massive kitchen island.

"I'll get the bottle." Adam pushed to his feet and crossed the kitchen.

Little Brittany was still at that age where she mostly slept the day away. Though originally bought for decoration, in the corner of the front parlor an antique cradle still worked great for a baby Brittany's size. That's where Becky found DJ.

"You okay?" she asked.

Staring at the small bundle, DJ nodded.

"Brooks still at the hospital?"

"Yeah." DJ continued to stare down at Brittany. "I hit Jake in the shoulder. Nothing serious, but he still had to go into surgery. Brooks wanted to stay until he wakes up. He's ordered more tests."

"What will happen to him?"

"It's in the county's hands now." DJ lifted his gaze to the ceiling and blew out a deep breath. "Charlotte kept apologizing for her husband. I can't understand how she can stand by him after what he did."

"Maybe it's *because* of what he did that she's standing by him."

DJ's head whipped around, his steely gaze landing on her. "The man could have killed her...and Meg."

"I know."

"Would you stay with a man like that?"

It took her a second to imagine what she might do if Ethan came home a changed man and became a threat to her and the people who cared about him. "I honestly don't know."

"I don't get it." DJ stepped back from the cradle then turned to face her. "You're thinking about Ethan aren't you?"

Her head bobbed once. "War does horrible things to some people."

This time DJ's chin dipped in agreement before turning back to the still sleeping baby and mumbling, "Hoorah."

"What's really bothering you?" she dared to ask.

DJ took a step back. "Everything and nothing."

"That covers a lot of territory."

"Yeah, it does." His weight shifted from one leg to the other as his hand rubbed his neck and fell to his side again. "I thought I left all this in Dallas, but shit follows you no matter what you do."

She had no idea how to answer that.

"Right this minute Charlotte is sitting dutifully at her husband's bedside. Her sister from Houston is next to her. Charlotte wants him to get better and come home and her sister wants him in jail."

"And you?"

"I keep thinking about the kind-hearted kid I knew in school and trying to picture him in jail." DJ shook his head. "Maybe I didn't do him any favors aiming for his shoulder."

The pain in his eyes drew Becky closer. Stopping beside him, she let her fingers fall on his arm. "You can't fix the world. None of us can."

His eyes met hers and she felt a sudden rush of energy surge between them. His gaze fell to where her hand rested on his arm and her fingers lifted at the unexpected heat.

"You two planning on staying out here all day?" Toni said as she came into the room. "I can't believe I'm going to have one of those soon."

DJ's gaze slowly lifted to meet Becky's and lingered an extra moment before he stepped back and turned to his sister-in-law and chuckled. "I can't believe my brother is going to have one of these soon."

The smile that graced Toni's lips didn't quite reach her eyes. Becky wasn't privy to the whole story between Brooks and Toni and her late husband and the rushed wedding and the yet to be officially announced pregnancy, but whatever it was, Becky felt sure it could be blamed for the shaky smile.

Still feeling the warmth of his skin on her fingertips, Becky clenched her fists and, facing Toni, forced a grin. "At least Brooks is better at diaper changing."

Toni's stuttered laugh broke the tension lingering in the small room. "Oh, he'd better get a lot better!"

"He will," Becky said, "we'll let him practice on Brittany again before we go home."

"Sounds like a plan." Toni's phone rang and reading the caller name, her face lit up. "Speak of the devil." She held up the phone a second before accepting the call and stepping out into the hall.

Becky's gaze followed Toni's disappearing form. "They really are very happy, aren't they?"

"Yeah. They are," DJ agreed.

All of a sudden the Farraday men were dropping off the town's most eligible bachelor list with surprising speed. Maybe there was something in the water?

• • • •

DJ loved his family. Really he did. But tonight he couldn't get away from the crowd and the questions fast enough. Any other time, when his support wasn't promised to a spunky woman and an abandoned baby, he'd have hunkered down behind his desk and tackled the mountain of paperwork and red tape that followed an officer firing a weapon. Instead, with an infant carrier in hand, he climbed the steps to what used to be his brother's apartment.

"I should give you a key." Becky slid past him to reach the front door.

The thought caught DJ by surprise. He was a guest. A key would be something more permanent. Glancing down at the baby, his thoughts sprinted in various directions. How long till the DNA results came back? What would happen when they did? What would he do if this little girl was his niece? If she wasn't?

Becky shoved the door open and stepped aside. "Home sweet home."

Again, her words surprised him. Home? He hadn't really had one of those since he'd left the ranch. Yeah, he had a place to park his butt and watch TV or crawl under the covers if he wasn't sacking out at the station, but home?

Placing her keys on a nearby hook, Becky spun about. "I suppose we could just leave her in the carrier till she wakes up hungry."

"You suppose?" DJ had followed Becky's lead so far. She'd seemed totally confident in her handling of the baby. Like she'd already raised a passel of her own.

Becky shrugged. "Hey, babysitting only gets you so far."

Since no one had ever asked him to babysit in his entire life, she was leaps and bounds ahead of him in the what-to-do-now department. "Where do I put her?"

"I suppose," she grinned before glancing away, "the bedroom should be fine."

"Bedroom it is." He'd set the carrier down on the floor beside the portable crib and smiled. Farraday or not, as far as babies went, this one was pretty sweet. He'd barely crossed the threshold when his gaze fell on Becky's derriere as she straightened by the fridge, a longneck brew in her hand.

"Thirsty?"

It took the saliva a few seconds to return to his mouth so he could form words. "That would be great. Thanks." Settled on the sofa, he dropped his ankle over his knee and drank back a long swallow. Not cool enough. "Aren't you having one?"

At the other end of the couch, reaching for the remote, she shook her head. "Never developed a taste for beer."

Did she keep the fridge stocked for someone else? Had she gotten back together with Ben? No, DJ had seen him and the schoolteacher having dinner at the café just the other night. "Why do you keep beer in the fridge if you don't like it?"

"Cause you do."

His booted foot fell to the floor with a thud. "What?"

"After a long day at the ranch, all y'all like to have a beer. Sometimes after dinner too."

DJ blinked. She was right. Whenever he worked with Finn and his brothers they often had a cold beer before supper, but it had been ages since Becky had been over at the ranch for dinner. "You remember that?"

She nodded.

He looked down at the label. His favorite. "When did you have time to pick this up?"

"There was a lull mid-morning and while everyone passed Brittany around I ran to pick up a few items."

"Like my favorite beer?"

Color tinged her cheeks and she shrugged it off. "I needed eggs and bread too."

And beer for him. Right about now, DJ was thinking it would be too easy to get used to a life like this. Comfy couch, cool drink, cute baby, and a beautiful, thoughtful woman. DJ blinked. Woman? His gaze settled on Becky. The same age as his little sister, Becky was seven years his junior. When he'd graduated high school she and Grace hadn't even hit the awkward teenage years. When he'd come back from the marines, he'd felt a hundred years older than when he'd left and Becky and Grace were in high school giggling and squealing at the strangest things. Even when he'd returned to Tuckers Bluff to take the job of Police Chief, though Becky was a legal adult, to him she was still the sweet kid who hung out with Grace. Hell, until a few days ago he still thought of her as another little sister. Even working with Adam perpetuated the lingering image of spunky kid next door who volunteered at the clinic on weekends because she loved animals. But there was so much more to Miss Rebecca Wilson.

How had he missed it? He'd always noticed she was kind and capable and even pretty. But all grown up she was strong, more than capable; she was bloody taking charge and kicking ass. The depths of her nurturing nature went well beyond cute kittens to championing for helpless babies and even soothing world weary men who had seen too much darkness in the world. She'd truly grown into one helluva woman. One in love with his brother. And didn't that just suck.

He downed another long swallow and forced his gaze away from Becky and over to the TV. She'd been flipping stations and stopped at an old movie channel. His mind darted back and forth through the scenes of the day. At least for a little while, thoughts of Becky had kept him from thinking about Jake and Charlotte and the fubar that situation had turned into. He should have known better. Should have seen it coming. Should have recognized Jake was a powder keg ready to explode—and take someone with him.

Instead of the soft gurgles that usually sounded when Brittany was waking, a sharp wail pierced the room. He and Becky were on their feet and bursting through the closed bedroom door. Red-faced and feet pumping, little Brittany was screaming her heart out.

"There, there," Becky cooed and cradled the baby against her shoulder. "I bet it was just a nasty dream."

Normally the baby would settle somewhat as soon as someone picked her up. Even when she was hungry and impatient, she never screeched like this.

"Should I get her bottle?" He knew it hadn't been that long since she'd been fed, but nothing else seemed to make her as happy as a warm bottle. What he didn't like was the slight crease forming between Becky's brows.

"I'll change her diaper. Maybe she pooped. Can't blame her for not wanting to stay in a dirty diaper."

DJ nodded. "One warm bottle coming up." He wasn't ready to deal with baby poop.

In the kitchen he went to task, waiting for the cries to stop. Or at least slow down. But nothing. The bottle was ready and Becky rocked her way across the room, cooing and swaying and bouncing, and Brittany wasn't having any of it.

"Let me try." He stretched out his arms and Becky's brows rose high on her forehead. He couldn't blame her for her reaction, even he was a little surprised to hear his own words. They'd tumbled out before his brain had had any time to filter the content. If Becky couldn't make Brittany happy, why the heck would he think he could?

"Sure." She surprised him, handing off the child. Immediately DJ found himself doing the same rocking, swaying and bouncing routine Becky had just gone through. His version wasn't working any better. "Try the bottle," she added.

Right. The bottle. Already feeling relief at the prospect of a quiet, happy baby, DJ tucked her into the crook of his arm and teased her lips with the rubber tipped bottle. If anything, she screamed louder seconds before vomiting up a stream of creamy white gunk. And he thought the first part of the day had been hell.

The next hour or so flew by in a blur. DJ rocked the baby. Becky paced with her. They took turns. After a couple of tries with the bottle only to have Brittany spit it all back up, they quickly gave up on that idea and went back to walking, rocking and even singing. Apparently "You Are My Sunshine" seemed to be a favorite tune with the cranky baby. DJ wondered if it was the melody or something her mother might have sung to her. His mind drifted back to the image of Brittany under a bench in a cardboard box and he decided no mother who could do that was likely to sing to her baby.

"Maybe we should call Brooks?" he suggested, feeling out of his depth and considerably unsettled.

Becky nibbled on her lower lip and DJ was struck with an unexpected urge to lean over and nibble on it too. "It's almost midnight."

"What good is having a brother for a doctor if you can't call him in the middle of the night?"

"I just hate to bother him after a day like today if it's just a normal baby spitting up thing." She went back to worrying that lower lip. "At least it's not coming out at both ends. I bet once she quiets down again she'll be fine."

"What do you think it is?"

Becky shook her head. "I'm not sure, but she seems to finally have nodded off."

So distracted by those lips, he hadn't even noticed that Brittany had fallen asleep on his shoulder. "Yeah, maybe the worst is behind us." He glanced at the still baby and back at Becky. "Should I try and lay her down."

Without hesitation, Becky's head swayed from side to side. "Not yet. Let's wait until she's seriously out cold."

He could go with that idea.

"Do you think this is why the mother left her?" Becky asked. "Because she fusses at night?"

"You mean tonight. She was fine last night." Well, at least for a couple of hours at a pop.

"True." Becky shook her head. "I know women abandon children all the time, but I just don't understand how."

DJ learned a long time ago to stop trying to understand the travesties of the world, but at the moment he was inclined to agree with Becky.

"Do you think Ethan will try to find her?" Becky reached forward and gently ran a finger down the baby's arm.

It took DJ a few seconds to realize Becky was referring to the mother, not the child and shook his head. "I've already got Brooklyn looking for her. Just in case."

"You do?" Becky's eyes rounded with surprise.

"She signed away her rights, but I want to make sure it's all on the up and up."

The light suddenly dimmed in Becky's eyes.

"Even if we find her," he continued quickly, "that doesn't mean Ethan will want to contact her."

"Who's to say he doesn't know how to find her already? Surely he must have her number or something?"

DJ blinked. How was he supposed to respond to that one? How did he explain to someone as sweet and kind as Becky that a marine on leave, especially one that has been living in a hellhole with a platoon of dirty tired men, doesn't particularly care what hole he sticks it in. The prettier the better, but after enough booze, even that doesn't matter anymore. Taking names and numbers was rarely part of the arrangement.

"I smell wood burning." The hint of a smile tugged at one side of her face.

"Excuse me?"

"You're thinking too hard. If that little line between your eyebrows gets any deeper, you'll hurt your brain."

"It's nothing."

"I don't believe that for a minute." She looked off toward the front window and then turned back to him. "You think I don't get it."

"I didn't say that."

She shrugged. "You didn't have to. Just because I choose not to dwell on what Ethan's life is like, doesn't mean I don't know about a girl in every port."

"That's sailors."

"So you're saying that Ethan is a pillar of virtue and this child is just an anomaly?"

Damn, he wished they'd go back to talking about fishing in the creek, the pros and cons of diaper brands, even about Jake Thomas.

"That bad?" She leaned back and crossed her legs Indian style. "I always picture Ethan exactly the way he appears on his social media accounts. Smiling, laughing, hanging out with his buddies. But I'm aware he's not a saint." A knowing smile curled her lips. "None of you brothers are."

DJ had never claimed to be a saint, but for some reason, having Becky call him out on perfectly normal adult relations had him wanting to squirm in his seat like a kid caught making out on the family sofa.

Her smile bloomed from cheek to cheek. "You're cute when you blush."

"Thanks. Cute was definitely the look I was going for."

"Declan James Farraday, cute is a compliment."

His efforts to hide the flinch at the use of his full name weren't fast enough and Becky rolled her eyes at him. "Any time Declan and James were used in the same sentence, I was inevitably in a lot of trouble. If Farraday was tacked on to the end, I could be taking my last breath."

"I don't think it was ever that bad. Besides," she shrugged, "I always thought calling you DJ was a waste of a beautiful name."

He'd been told a lot of different things about his name. Especially in the marines where playing with people's names was as normal during a tour of duty as eating popcorn at the movies. He was just grateful some of the less than flattering plays on his name hadn't stuck. Going through four years of the marines with the handle Duckland would have changed the game. "Thank you. For what it's worth, I've always thought Rebecca suited you. It's a lovely name."

A charming shade of pink singed Becky's cheeks. Any color looked lovely on her. For his own good, he figured it was time to move on.

Brittany hadn't stirred and he hoped that meant they were past the worst of it. "Let's see if I can get her down so we can get a little shuteye."

Becky nodded and slowly they made their way into the bedroom. DJ did his best to pass the baby from his shoulder to his hands and into the portable crib. Standing perfectly still, waiting for an ear-piercing scream if Brittany didn't intend to spend the night, DJ held his breath. Satisfied the baby was going to stay sound asleep, he took a step back. Becky inched away as well when Brittany shifted her bottom up into the air and exercised her lungs.

"And here we go around." DJ scooped the baby up, laid her against his shoulder and proceeded to pace and rock. This longest day of his life just didn't want to end.

CHAPTER ELEVEN

Struggling to open her eyes, Becky flinched at the pain shooting down her neck and across her left shoulder. She'd been dreaming about a big empty field of hay except for a big old bull, an unsteady new calf and a half naked cowboy. Blinking her eyes quickly, the morning fog in her brain was slowly clearing and her mind was waking up. She wasn't in a field with a bull or any other animal, she was in the middle of her living room curled up on the loveseat and...oh yeah.

Springing up, she looked to the bedroom door before noticing DJ on the sofa across from her. Still in his pants, he'd stripped out of his t-shirt the last time Brittany spat up on him. Which might explain the crazy dream. At one end of the couch his booted feet hung over the top, at the opposite end his head lolled forward, his chin touching his chest. She wasn't going to be the only one with a painful crimp in her neck.

The culprit responsible for the loss of sleep and tantalizing dreams that would have given Freud a laugh, lay nestled in the crook of DJ's arm.

By somewhere around three in the morning, she and DJ had once again returned to pacing and rocking Brittany to sleep one last time and Becky and DJ must have nodded off too, because she couldn't remember anything else after that.

Now she watched the gentle giant sleeping with the precious baby. Most of her life, she'd envisioned moments exactly like this, only with Ethan. The handsome fair-haired brave daredevil would put away his expensive toys and come home to set down roots. Not that flying missions in the military was a game, it was dangerous as hell and she knew that. Even now, her stomach churned with unease almost every day knowing one of those missions was most likely why Ethan hadn't responded to any of his brothers' recent attempts to contact him. But for the first time, watching DJ sleeping with his arm protectively cradling Brittany, Ethan's baby, circumstance chiseled away at her warped perspective of reality. Ethan's baby being the startling key. At no point was she stupid enough to think Brittany was the divine conception. Despite the baffled way DJ had looked at her, she didn't believe Ethan ignored the opposite sex, she simply chose not to think about how much of their company he might enjoy. Not till last night, over a few quiet moments' conversation and the strained expressions dancing across DJ's face, did she understand exactly how many women were most likely involved in Ethan's real world. At least when on leave.

Both she and DJ were a little punch drunk from lack of sleep by the time Brittany had fallen into her first deep sleep of the night. Somewhere, the words barfly and hookup were used a time too many for her own comfort, and she realized DJ's comments about Aunt Eileen's potential fear of how many other children had Ethan fathered wasn't quite the joke she'd taken it to be.

And that was when reality hit. The kind, sweet, charming man she'd adored since he'd come to her rescue in the first grade, had probably slept with every attractive willing woman to cross his path. Well, maybe not every, but from the pitiful way DJ had looked at Becky, she'd guessed *every* wasn't that far off the mark.

Slowly padding across the room, she moved cautiously through the kitchen wanting to allow DJ as much sleep as possible. Measuring coffee, she made it strong the way he liked it and then tossed in an extra scoop. They were both going to need it. By her calculations, the last nap had lasted a full two hours giving her a grand total of maybe three hours sleep, if that. From where she stood, DJ looked to be dead to the world. So much so, if she hadn't known what they'd been through the night before, she would have checked his pulse to see if he had indeed died in his sleep.

The smart thing to do now would be catch a very quick shower while the coffee brewed, the problem being she was having a really hard time dragging her eyes away from DJ's naked chest. The man wore a shirt really well. Anyone knew that. At more than one girl's night out, there had been joking and teasing about what great asses all the brothers had too. Tall, dark and hunky rolled off the tongue when speaking of a Farraday, but the last time she'd seen any of the Farradays without a shirt, she'd been a little girl and they had been pretty gangly teens. Boy, had things changed.

Strong muscled arms still held on tightly to Brittany. Strength that came from hard work and healthy exercise. A splattering of dark curly hair spread from nipple to nipple. Just enough for a girl to let her fingers wander. Those same dark hairs trailed down his middle, swirled around his belly button and disappeared in a V by his undone buckle. The man definitely knew how to wear sexy. And wasn't she just as bad as those barflies, staring unabashedly at the sleeping man on her sofa.

"Mornin'." His voice came out low and rough and made the hairs on her arms stand at attention.

Eyes wide open, his gaze shifted to the kitchen. How long had he been awake? Had he seen her staring at him? At his chest? Dear God, at his...buckle? Desperate to run and hide for getting caught gawking, she screwed up her courage, praying she wasn't blushing like a virtuous schoolgirl, and lowered her voice to a whisper, "I'm making coffee."

His voice dropped even lower. "Bless you."

She chuckled softly. The nice side of this crazy situation was getting to know the funny, easy going part of DJ she hadn't known over morning coffee, late night conversation and even old movies. When she and Grace were young, he was just older. When he moved home after serving in the marines and working in Dallas, he always seemed the serious adult. She admired his attitude, his service, his respectability, but she *liked* this side of DJ.

Placing his free hand at the back of Brittany's head, DJ slowly swung his legs around and eased himself to sitting position.

"Shall I take her?" Becky hurried around the sofa to stand in front of him.

"I need to use the bathroom."

Nodding, she carefully slid the baby into her arms. Brittany stirred and shifted and for a few seconds Becky was afraid the fussing and crying would start all over, but the infant settled into her shoulder and both she and DJ let out an audible sigh.

With a dip of his chin and a smile, he took a step forward and rolled his neck from side to side. She knew she shouldn't, but Becky kept her eyes on his back as he crossed the room. From any angle, the man was just fine. And wasn't she just awful for once again gawking. She seriously needed to get a man of her own.

• • • •

Damn. At the bathroom sink, DJ splashed cool water in his face and blew out several long deep breaths. What he needed was a long, icy shower. Never had he been so thankful for the restraint of good old-fashioned denim. When he woke up thinking of Becky only to find her staring at him, every inch of his skin tightened with the sensation of her gaze scanning over him as though her soft hands had covered him instead. The only thing that had kept old glory from standing at full embarrassing attention was knowing even though her eyes stared in his direction, the one on her mind had to be Ethan. Ethan and his baby.

Besides, now wasn't the time to get all bent out of a shape by a woman. Especially not this woman. He had one hell of a day ahead of him with the Thomas shooting, and following up on the DNA samples, and a sweet sick baby to contend with. Brittany, of course, was the priority. Brushing his teeth and closing his buckle, he looked down at his bare chest. Last night, Brittany had gone through the few clean t-shirts he'd brought with him. At some point today, stopping by his place for more clothes was going to have to be squeezed onto the mile long to-do list. And definitely more t-shirts than he would normally need. Taking a minute, he swung into the bedroom and pulled out a clean uniform shirt. He was still buttoning it when he came to a stop in the short hall. Able to see and hear Becky softly singing to the tiny sleeping baby, his heart stuttered. Ethan was a lucky son of a bitch—if he'd open his eyes and see what was right in front of him. A sweet baby and a woman who didn't question how that baby got here.

He forced his feet to move forward. In DJ's line of work, he didn't think often of home and hearth, but right about now, having a woman love him and his baby seemed like an awfully sweet dream.

• • • •

"So what's the verdict?" Becky asked.

"Hard to say for sure." Brooks closed up his medical bag. Being dragged out of bed just after six in the morning after a day and night like yesterday wasn't his favorite thing to do, especially not now that Toni slept snuggly beside him. "Mild signs of flaky skin, a few red patches and the vomiting. My suspicion is she's allergic to the formula you bought her."

"I didn't know." Becky whispered softly, looking to the baby. DJ, on the other hand, looked to Becky. Concern filled both their gazes. *Interesting.* Not that it would surprise him that DJ would worry over the health of any baby, but the unease in his gaze seemed clearly directed at Becky, not the baby. And wasn't that a different development.

"So what do we do now?" DJ asked.

"Most infant allergies are caused by a protein in a cow milk based formula. I'm not sure what formulas the sisters have. You could try a soy based formula. About 15% of babies allergic to milk based formula will be allergic to soy based formula so the odds are 85% in her favor."

"And if she's one of the 15%?"

"There are a couple of other formula options. I have samples of two different ones at the clinic but you'll probably have to go to Butler Springs to stock up." He snapped his case shut. "Give her some water now to keep her tummy full. I'm sure either Sister or Sissy will be delighted to open up early if you give them a call."

"Thanks. Appreciate you coming over so early."

Brooks laughed. House calls wouldn't happen if he'd stayed in Dallas, but he wouldn't trade his lifestyle here for anything short of a cure for cancer. And… "Next time don't wait till morning to call."

DJ reached out and Becky handed the baby over. No one said a word. DJ patted Brittany's back and walked into the kitchen, Becky turned toward the door. It took Brooks a few seconds to gather his thoughts and follow Becky. Only a couple of nights and these two had fallen into a seamless routine that included silent communication. Oh hell yes, this was getting very interesting.

CHAPTER TWELVE

"**G**o take a nap. That's an order." Adam tossed a file on the counter top and shook his head at Becky. "Seriously, you look like an audition for the Walking Dead. We can handle things here."

More than once this morning, Becky had dozed off at her desk only to have the weight of her own head snap her awake again. At least twice she'd given Adam the wrong patient file. How she'd confused an aging feline named Gertrude with a young canine named Max, she had no idea. Not the numbers, letters or folder colors were anything close to each other.

So far, it seemed the new formula sat well with Brittany, but Becky had let Kelly and the lab techs take turns feeding the baby for fear she'd fall asleep and drop the poor thing.

"See, you're too tired to even answer. Go." Adam urged her on.

"The baby—"

"Is well cared for. Spoiled even. Go."

"You're a good boss." The words that past her lips sounded something like "Yogle Bows," but either Adam didn't notice or didn't care. Now all she had to do was put one foot in front of the other and climb the stairs. Never had the thought of bed seemed so wonderful. She had no idea how parents lived and worked and raised children—more than one of them—every day, but she was more than ready to turn little Brittany over to her full time parents. Half way to the front door she paused by the porta crib and peeked in on the sleeping baby. *Or maybe not.*

• • • •

"I don't like this." Reed stood at DJ's side in his office.

"You don't have to like it. It is what it is." Standard Operating Procedure. All police involved shooting incidents had to be investigated whether in the far reaches of West Texas or a metropolitan madhouse like Dallas. Administrative leave was unavoidable. In the case of a department the size of Tuckers Bluff, DJ would be doing his job from his desk—most of his job. "Besides, it's not like I don't spend a good chunk of the day in this seat anyhow."

"You didn't yesterday." Hands behind his back, Reed stood at parade rest. Some marine habits were harder to break than others.

"Which is why we're waiting for an investigator to declare things business as usual." DJ hated this part of the job, but he wasn't about to let on to his officer. Waiting to find out if you still *had* a job or would be facing trial thanks to a stubborn DA, media with an agenda, or witnesses who couldn't keep a family portrait straight never mind the details of a gun battle in a panic filled moment. At least here and now, none of those issues should come into play. The incident was cut and clear, the witnesses all would be fine. Hopefully sooner than later.

Reed shifted his weight, his stance more relaxed. "Any idea how long it'll take?"

"A few days. A few weeks. Who the hell knows." DJ heard the frustration in his voice and forced his shoulders to relax, immediately feeling some of the tension leave his body. Not that he didn't still have a shit ton of crap on his plate. In Dallas, he'd be home watching the plants grow. At least here, he could keep doing most of his job. The only difference being, unlike yesterday, if all hell broke loose again for the second time in decades, Reed would be the one calling the shots. "I figure I'll spend this afternoon filling out forms until my fingers fall off. Hopefully this will all be over with sooner than later."

"Old man Thomas came in to town to open the feed store."

The tension in his shoulders was back. "You might want to keep an extra eye on the place. The old goat won't take kindly to the gossip and looky-loos." Now might be a good time for DJ to pick up an order from the feed store for Finn, or place it if necessary. "Any word on Jake and Charlotte?" The first thing he'd asked Brooks this morning was for an update on Jake. *Stable* was the only thing Brooks would say. DJ was set to meet with both Adam and Brooks at the café shortly. Not that he had much to report, but it was something they did when they could and this morning, he not only could, he needed to. Turning his wrist, he confirmed the time. "I'll be at the Silver Spurs if you've got any questions." He paused and looked around the office that had been his domain since leaving Dallas. "She's all yours."

Jaw clenched tightly, Reed nodded.

Yeah, buddy. DJ knew exactly how the guy felt. He'd learned a long time ago there was no controlling everything in life, but right about now, he'd certainly like for just one thing in life to go the way it should.

Normally, DJ would have hopped into the squad car to drive the short distance from the station to the café, but until the investigation into the Thomas shooting was over, DJ couldn't respond to any police business that didn't involve his desk and computer. Besides, exercise was good for him. He reminded himself of that tidbit with every step until reaching the front door.

"How's my guy?" Spotting him from across the café, Abbie hurried to greet him.

DJ didn't bother with words, he simply nodded. He and Abbie went back a long way. Longer than when she'd rolled into town looking for work—and peace of mind.

Stopping in front of him, Abbie grabbed a couple of menus and used the time to study his face. Since no one from Tuckers Bluff had actually looked at a menu since they were first printed back when Frank came on as cook, he knew what she was doing. After stalling as long as she could without drawing attention to herself, she must have decided he wasn't about to wig out on anyone because she nodded back and signaled for him to follow.

"Your brothers are back here with their wives. You may need to mediate. Toni looks spitting mad."

Glancing ahead, DJ didn't know if he should laugh or turn tail and run. He was pretty sure any second now fire would come pouring from Toni's nose and steam from her ears. "What has her all riled up?"

"What always riles a woman up? Money and men. Lethal combination." She shoved the menu at him and waving to the table with a little extra flourish, smiled and turned back to her other waiting customers.

Now that he was close enough to see the whites of everyone's eyes, he was almost positive he should run for the hills. There was no winning an argument, and that's what it looked like, if it was the women against the men. Surely, after years of watching their parents and then his Aunt Eileen, Brooks had learned if the lady of the house ain't happy, nobody's happy. "Should I come back later?" It was a chicken's question, but a key survival instinct was living to see another day.

"No," four voices roused at him.

He grabbed an empty chair from a nearby table and pulled it up to the end. "Do I want to know why you all look like someone put gravel in your grits?"

"Your brother is beyond bullheaded." Toni crossed her arms and leaned back in her seat. This was the first time DJ could think of seeing these two anything less than happily hovering.

"It's not bullheaded. It's not my money."

"That's right." Toni leaned forward again. "It's mine now and I can do what I want with it. Or at least some of it!"

DJ looked left then right, immediately noticing Adam and Meg were suspiciously quiet.

"You tell her." Brooks waved a finger from DJ to Toni.

"I plead the fifth. Especially since I have no idea what you two are arguing about."

Brooks blew out a long breath. "After I left you and Becky this morning, I drove over to Butler Springs to check on Jake."

"Which, if we had a small clinic here in town, you wouldn't have to do."

"I'm not a general surgeon."

Toni leaned back again. DJ could tell from the way her fingers tapped against her elbow she wasn't buying it. "But in an emergency you could have done it, couldn't you?"

Another heavy breath escaped from DJ's brother. "Yes."

"And if the town had a clinic you'd have gotten that MRI on Jake sooner wouldn't you?"

"There's no telling." Brooks shook his head. "It might not have made any difference at all."

"Okay, I'll agree there, but today would be easier on everyone, including Charlotte, if Jake were having his tests here."

"Tests?" DJ asked.

"We did an MRI this morning. I suspected there was a physiological problem with Jake, but couldn't get him into Butler Springs."

"And...?" Meg urged, speaking up for the first time since DJ's arrival.

Brooks ran two fingers up and down the side of his temple. Exhaustion taking over his face.

"You know Charlotte's going to tell us when we get there this afternoon anyhow," Meg insisted.

"You have heard of HIPAA laws?" Brooks let his hand fall to his side.

"Oh for heaven's sake, we're not going to report you and neither is Charlotte," Toni huffed.

Brooks turned to DJ. "You're going to hear about it soon too."

DJ didn't mention that he was currently a little further down the chain of command then he'd been yesterday.

"Jake's got a brain tumor. Based on its size and location, it may very well explain the growing fits of violence."

"Operable?" Adam asked.

"I'm not a neurosurgeon—"

Toni's lips tightened as she glared at her husband. It was clear to everyone at the table that as far as she was concerned, her husband could walk on water and perform any surgery with his hands tied behind his back.

"—but my guess is yes. And before you ask, if the tumor is the cause for the anger, Jake could return to normal."

"Well, thank God for that." Meg nodded, a whisper of a smile gracing her features.

"Which brings us back to the clinic here in Tuckers Bluff." Toni's expression softened. "If someone else offered to start a building fund you'd jump on it."

This time Brooks' jaw tightened and DJ knew Toni was hitting a nerve.

"Okay, I'll risk life and limb. Exactly what has you two squabbling?" DJ asked.

Toni turned to face him. "William's life insurance check cleared my bank. I want to put some money away for college tuition for the baby, but I want to start a clinic fund with the rest."

Now DJ got it. He looked straight at Brooks. "If the money came from anywhere else in town, what would you say then?" Damn simple question, but it needed to be asked by someone besides the person offering the money.

Brooks looked across the table to Adam. The oldest Farraday brother shrugged. Meg did the same as Brooks' gaze shifted back from Adam to DJ. "I guess I'd start looking for land."

"And there we have my other point." Toni took a sip of water. "I bumped into Mrs. Rogers in front of the Cut and Curl this morning. She mentioned that after yesterday, Mr. Rogers decided to stop putting off retirement and move to someplace warm all year round with more things for old people to do than rock on the porch and listen to their arteries harden."

Meg turned to Adam. "Which is the Roger's place?"

"The antebellum house just outside of town." Adam looked to Brooks, no doubt thinking exactly what DJ was. That old place would make a great small town hospital, never mind clinic.

"Actually," Toni said, "it's more Georgian with all that brick, but it probably was built in the antebellum period."

All heads spun in Toni's direction.

"Hey," Toni shrugged casually, "I took a few historical architecture classes so my brain wouldn't explode from all the math."

Meg shook her head, her eyes crossed in confusion. "Don't you have to do math to do architectural drawings?"

"Not the same math as accounting. Design is way more fun." Toni rubbed her hands together and smiled. "So, am I right or am I right?"

DJ looked to his brother and crossed his arms with a grin. To his left he could see Adam doing the same. Poor Brooks was outnumbered. And when Aunt Eileen found out what Toni wanted to do, there would be a wooden sign in the middle of town with a red thermometer measuring donations for all the fundraisers the town was about to be bombarded with before Brooks could mutter a protest. Yep, for all that was going wrong in the Farraday family, when it came to spunky women, some things were going very right.

CHAPTER THIRTEEN

*H*oly... Four hours. Becky swore she would only lie down for twenty minutes. A power nap. She'd even set her alarm. And slept through it. Springing up from bed as though the house were haunted and the Ghost of Christmas Past was on her heels, she looked around for her shoes before noticing she'd never bothered to take them off.

So dang tired, she'd shuffled into the bedroom and flopped onto the mattress. What must everyone think of her abandoning that little baby for hours? Well, maybe not abandoning, but certainly shirking her responsibilities. Hurrying into the bathroom, she rinsed sleep breath from her mouth and then grabbed the keys and bolted out the door, sprinting down the stairs to the vet clinic.

Trotting around to the back door, the place seemed awfully peaceful for somewhere usually filled with sounds of miscellaneous animals, their owners, and the employees going about their business. Not till she reached the front offices did she make the connection. Adam had cleared his afternoon schedule to meet with his brothers. The lab techs had closed all doors to the kennel room and the entire staff was huddled around Brittany. "Did anyone get any work done today?"

"Nope." Kelly grinned. "It's almost like being a grandparent. All the fun and none of the responsibility."

"We're just doing our part to keep things quiet," Pat, one of the lab techs, added. "When we're out here, all the kennel pets don't raise the roof."

"Yeah," Kelly added, "out of sight, out of mind."

Is that how the mother left her baby behind? Out of sight out of mind? "Well, thanks for the break. I was more tired than I thought."

"And just think," Kelly pointed to the baby in Pat's arms, "how tired you'd be doing this for a few years if she were yours."

"Well, she's not, so that's a moot point." And why did those words sting? Becky wasn't in any hurry to have kids. Like every little girl growing up, she'd dreamed of the romance and magic of falling in love. Expected to have a couple of years with her husband before starting a family. Fun, happy years like Adam and Meg seemed to be having whenever she saw them. Drinking in the besotted look on her husband's face much the same as the look on any of the three older Farraday men when they looked at their women. The way she'd always pictured Ethan would look at her as soon as he noticed she wasn't just the skinny girl next door. Except taking care of Brittany these last couple of days must have worn her out more than she'd realized. The dreams and visions of her and Ethan were cloudy and fuzzy and felt like they were slipping away.

Then again, how could she lose someone she'd never had?

• • • •

"Charlotte and her sister are staying in a motel, but we promised we'd stop by today." Standing at the corner table, Toni leaned over and kissed her husband, her eyes searching his and smiling at the love reflected back at her. Hell, anyone looking at the guy could tell he adored his wife even if she'd just bested him in a disagreement.

"Meant to get an earlier start." Meg kissed her husband softly on the lips. "Looks like we'll be grabbing supper with Charlotte in Butler Springs. Will you be all right on your own?"

Adam nodded and, just for good measure, pulled Meg into his arms for a slightly more fervent locking of lips.

DJ coughed. "Just a reminder, there are other people in the café."

Meg let her forehead rest a second on Adam's and then, stepping around DJ, slapped him on the shoulder. "Have you considered getting a girl of your own? You're not getting any younger you know."

Served him right for speaking up. Though lately, a girl of his own crept into his thoughts—and under his skin—more often than was prudent. Not wanting to talk about his administrative leave, or the upcoming investigation, or even how all the latest discoveries would affect the entire mess, DJ opted to bring up the other complication in their lives. "Brooklyn forwarded me an email from the DNA lab confirming receipt of the samples. Both are good to go."

"How long will it be till we get the results?" Adam asked.

"Brooklyn says we might have them as early as tomorrow."

Brooks whistled. "Oh, this guy either has some sweet connections or he's lying through his teeth."

"I'd go with sweet connections. I'm pretty sure we got bumped to the top of the list."

Adam opened his mouth to say something, snapped it shut, looked around, and then pressing forward, whispered over the table. "Let's take the rest of this conversation back to my office."

Brooks and DJ both nodded and pushed to their feet. At the register, the brothers paid the tabs and, hat in hand, DJ placed his on his head, tipped it at Abbie, and followed his brothers across the street to the vet clinic.

"You know," Adam looked over his shoulder as he led the way, "the Rogers place isn't in town the way you wanted, but you could probably get the building and immediate grounds for a song and let Larry Rogers sell the rest of the land off to the highest taker."

"Not many people want a big, old rambling house like that. I don't think all those rooms have been used in generations," DJ added.

"I get it, guys. I'll admit a time or two I've thought the same thing about that old place, but I never thought Larry would be interested in selling."

"Why not?" Adam pulled the clinic door open. "None of his kids are ranchers. I can't remember the last time I saw the whole brood come in for the holidays."

"That's right." DJ stepped over the threshold. "Didn't they all take a cruise or something last Christmas?"

"Yep." Brooks nodded. "And Larry paid for it."

"See." Adam took off his hat. "I'm thinking bargain basement price tag."

Huddled at the reception desk, all the women turned at the three brothers' entrance.

Adam pointed down the hall. "We'll be in my office."

"Looks like the new formula agrees with her?" Brooks paused by Becky and took in the happy baby.

"Seems so," Becky said, "though I've been upstairs sleeping."

Adam smiled. "You look better."

"Gee, thanks." Becky flashed a sassy smile and DJ's gut did a somersault.

He seriously needed to get a grip on his reactions to Becky. Ethan's Becky. Slowing at her side, DJ noticed the color had returned to Brittany's cheeks and her eyes seemed clear and alert again. Good. Seeing the baby feeling better brightened his otherwise crappy day. And wasn't that another unexpected twist. Which meant one more thing to add to the upcoming conversation.

Inside the office and with the door closed, Adam took a seat behind his desk. DJ plopped in a guest chair and looked up at his brother. "We know if Brittany's a Farraday she should be with Ethan—"

"If he's willing to separate from the corps and stay home," Adam said.

Brooks shrugged and shook his head. "Lots of servicemen and women have families while deployed. Ethan doesn't have to leave to get custody."

"We all know that whether or not Ethan stays," DJ looked pointedly at each of his siblings, "if Brittany is a Farraday, she'll be taken care of."

Both Brooks and Adam nodded.

"My question," he continued, "is what do we do if the mother lied? What happens if that cute little baby the whole town is falling for isn't Ethan's?"

All gazes bounced back and forth before Adam leaned back and sighed. "Do you really think she's not Ethan's?"

DJ shook his head. "I honestly don't know. I've got some preliminaries on the mother. Brooklyn is digging deeper. So far I already know she's a real piece of work. At fifteen, she was picked up for shoplifting, joy riding, and once for being in a motor vehicle with open containers of alcohol. Ran away from home at sixteen. Married at seventeen, divorced at eighteen. Fell off the grid for a few years until she showed up in California."

"And then?" Brooks asked.

"A couple of DWIs, some unpaid traffic tickets in Chula Vista, near San Diego. One arrest for possession, but no conviction. Really good lawyer."

"Who paid for that?" Adam asked.

"Police reports don't give that kind of information. It's why Brooklyn is still looking into her."

Adam rested his elbows on his desk. "What about family?"

"Her parents are dead. Juvenile reports list an aunt."

Brooks steepled his hands. "So you think she's lying?"

"I'm thinking she's the kind of gal who probably knew how to have a good time."

"And has enough of a conscience to pick a nice guy for the father?" Adam leaned back. "Doesn't fit."

Brooks nodded at his older brother. "On leave, one sailor is as nice as any other. The only reason Ethan would stand out in a crowd is if someone took the time to do a little internet search."

"Farraday Ranch," Adam and DJ echoed.

Brooks tapped the edge of his nose with his index finger. "Ding ding ding. Give the man a prize."

"Which brings us right back to where we started. What do we do if Brittany's not a Farraday?"

CHAPTER FOURTEEN

With Brittany contentedly napping in the break room, the veterinary staff had no choice but to return to some semblance of real work. Even with a long nap of her own, Becky still felt as though she'd been running full steam ahead with no reprieve, and with DJ, Adam, and Brooks behind closed doors, concentrating on the task at hand wasn't going well. A part of her kept expecting Connor and Finn to show up. Another part of her wondered if she'd be invited in. Of course, just because she'd been included in the discussion about Brittany the other night didn't mean she'd be included now. Then again, she was assuming the private meeting was about the baby. For all Becky knew, the gathering could be over anything from Connor's upcoming business plans and wedding to the crazy situation with Jake and Charlotte Thomas.

The door to Adam's office inched open and Becky immediately looked up.

"You sure you don't want to head to the ranch for supper with us?" First out the door, Brooks spoke to DJ over his shoulder.

"Nope. Y'all know everything I do. Just let me know what Connor and Finn have to say."

Brooks nodded and slapped his brother on the back. They all seemed perfectly calm, almost jovial. That would certainly indicate more pleasant topics of conversation had been discussed, like Connor and his soon to be new family.

Breaking apart from the pack, Adam came to a stop beside Kelly. "I'm heading out early. Going to the ranch. Y'all can cut lose any time."

Sticking her thumb straight up, Kelly smiled. "Got it."

Returning the smile, Adam tapped his Aggie ring on the counter top and turned for the door.

A few more back slaps and nods and DJ deviated away from his siblings and crossed to where Becky worked. "I'll take care of supper tonight."

"It's fine if you'd rather go with your brothers to the ranch." She pointed at Adam and Brooks, walking out the door.

"Nope. Staying in town."

Becky hesitated a moment than nodded. He was a big boy, allowed to do whatever he wanted. "As soon as Brittany wakes up, I'll be going home."

"Sounds good." DJ pushed away from the counter. The way he lingered, she thought he had something else to say, but all he did was nod and leave in his brothers' wakes.

Almost an hour later, Brittany was wide-awake and entertaining herself with cute noises and blowing an infant version of spit bubbles. Other than the night tech responsible for the animals boarding or recovering from surgery, Becky was the last staff person still in the clinic. Claiming a hot date, Kelly had escaped out the door mere moments after their boss. Her curvaceous friend had met a guy the last time they'd hit the Boot n Scoots for girl's night and things seemed to be clicking. Growing up, Kelly had been what Becky's grandmother called pleasingly plump. Others chose less flattering adjectives. Kelly still carried a few extra pounds but they'd balanced out in curves that more than enough men seemed to appreciate. Including this new cowboy in her life. Though Becky had no idea who she was going to hang out with on dateless Saturday nights if things with Kelly and her new cowboy got serious. But Becky was happy for her friend.

As for Pat, the senior lab tech had stuck around a bit longer waiting for her shift replacement before heading home. On her own, Becky had packed up and was merely waiting for Brittany to wake up. "Come on sweetheart."

Carrier slung over one arm and her handbag over the other shoulder, Becky couldn't move fast enough. Brittany was a pretty patient baby. Normally, when she wasn't as sick as a drunken sailor, the baby liked to look around and reach for nearby things, entertaining herself until hunger got the better of her disposition. Tonight's easygoing nature bolstered Becky's impressions that the worst of the formula fiasco was behind them.

In the back of Becky's mind, she clung to the idea that the longer Brittany entertained herself between feedings, the longer she might sleep at night without waking up hungry. It was a long shot, but after two nights of limited sleep, long shots grew exponentially in appeal.

The second she walked through her front door, the appetizing aromas of warm food slammed into her. "Oh wow. You didn't tell me you could cook." She kicked the door shut behind her.

"I can't. Well, actually I can, but most of what I make comes off a grill or out of a pot of boiling water."

"A pasta man, are you?" She laughed at his expression of mock surprise and then her stomach did that flutter thing when a sweet smile settled on his face.

"Man cannot live by bread alone, but rib eye or spaghetti works for me."

Her salivary glands warned her that whatever the meal, it would be delicious. Working to place the familiar scents, she took another sniff. "Oh my, is that Frank's lasagna?"

"It is." Lobster potholders on each hand, DJ looked absolutely adorable. All he needed to complete the handsome cowboy in the kitchen look was an oversize apron. "I also have fresh salad, warm garlic bread, and cheesecake for dessert."

"Oh, my. I've died and gone to heaven."

DJ chuckled. "I stopped at the café for the meatloaf, but when I saw lasagna on the specials board, I remembered how much you loved it when my aunt made lasagna."

Becky stopped halfway across the room. "You remembered I love lasagna?"

"Sure." He shrugged. "You loved her lasagna and her corned beef and cabbage. Corned beef wasn't on the café menu."

"And when it is, it's not as good as your aunt's." Becky's heart was doing a jig. Had anyone she'd ever known, never mind dated, remembered her favorite foods? "You like ketchup on your rice." She didn't know why she felt the need to share what she remembered from her youth about DJ.

He set the potholders down on the counter and tipping his head, shot back, "Your favorite ice cream is Butter Pecan."

"That's right." A perverse pleasure soared inside her. She set the carrier down, unbuckled the baby, and looked over her shoulder at DJ. "I don't remember you having a favorite ice cream flavor—"

"Because I'm an equal opportunity ice cream lover." Eyes twinkling with humor, he moved in her direction.

"But I do remember German Chocolate Cake." She bit back a laugh. "And the time you and Connor sliced—and ate—your Aunt Eileen's cake entry for the county fair."

"Ooh." DJ winced. "I don't think we sat comfortably for weeks."

"She was pretty ticked off."

"And then some."

Watching the two of them from her carrier seat, Brittany must have decided she'd had enough of the lighthearted banter. Her arms waved and her feet pumped. Becky had come to recognize that as the feed-me-now-or-I'm-going-to-scream routine. "I'd better get her bottle ready."

"Let me." DJ slipped passed her and lifted the baby into his arms. "Hey there, sweetie pie."

Becky couldn't drag her attention away from the interaction. When DJ smiled at the tiny baby, his entire face lit up. Little lines appeared at the corners of eyes sparkling with amusement. Holding her snuggly against him in one arm, he wiggled a single finger in front of her.

"You look much happier today, don't you?" he chatted to the baby.

Becky wasn't totally sure, but from where she stood, it looked like Brittany had just bestowed her first smile, at least in Tuckers Bluff, on Declan James Farraday. Once again, the infant pumped her feet and swinging an arm, five tiny fingers latched onto his still moving finger. Becky's heart nearly stopped at the precious moment, but if she thought DJ was delighted before, he was absolutely beaming now. If his reaction were electricity, he'd be a powerhouse. At that moment, his gaze shifted in Becky's direction and her heart did an honest to God back flip. Damn, was there anything sexier than a grinning man with a baby in his arms?

• • • •

"Not as good as your Aunt Eileen's, but dang close."

DJ watched the way Becky's lips closed around the last morsel of pasta on the fork, then oh-so-slowly she dragged the utensil out of her mouth, closed her eyes, and softly moaned. All he could do was shift in place and thank the stars her plate was empty.

The truth was, the fork probably slid in and out of her moist mouth much faster than his mind watched it play out, and her soft mewls of culinary pleasure were also exaggerated by his depraved mind. The reality of being in close quarters with this woman three nights in a row was way past getting to him. The conversation had meandered from Meg and Toni standing by Charlotte Thomas, what the results of Jake's MRI would mean for his legal case, to the baby's new formula and how could the mother have not left instructions with important details like a formula allergy. At least if the woman had left them the original formula container, they could have purchased the same brand.

Who knew sharing dinner and casual conversation, night after night, could make a man want a woman more than the sexiest bikini or sultriest banter. At least with this woman. Every bite Becky took had been sheer torture for him. A time or two she'd had to repeat herself because his mind had wandered down a path it had no business being on. The crazy thing was, if he did find a way to sneak off out of town to keep company with a female friend, it wouldn't do him any good. All he seemed to have a taste for was the one woman in town he shouldn't even be looking at this way.

"Do I remember hearing something about cheesecake?" With her napkin she wiped at the corners of her mouth.

"Yes, you did." Resisting the urge to stretch out his hand and swipe at the dab of sauce on one end of her mouth, he pushed back from the table. "You missed a spot."

She smiled, wiping her face again. "Thanks."

"No problem. I'll get the cheesecake." Distraction was a good thing.

"No." She pushed to her feet and almost slammed into him, losing her balance.

"Careful." Before he could think twice, his hands curled around her arms, holding her in place. "You okay?"

"I, uh…" Her gaze locked with his at the same moment her mouth snapped shut then fell open again. "Uhm." The tip of her tongue peeked out and quickly slid back into her mouth as she sucked in her bottom lip.

DJ desperately wanted to suck on that sweet lip for her. And a few other places too. *Blast.* He released his hold, keeping his open hands nearby, making sure she had her balance again.

"I, uh, should… I mean, you should…uh, let me get the dessert. I mean cheesecake."

DJ nodded. If he dared open his mouth to speak, he would no doubt bring it crashing down on hers and that was so not a good idea. Sucking in a deep breath, he took a step back. "Fair enough." Not that any of this was fair. Some days he wished his father had raised a house of scoundrels. But Sean Farraday had raised men by a standard. Respect. Honor. And the thoughts running through his mind were none of the above. She was too young, too long in love with his brother, and too good a friend to his sister. So many rules begging to be broken. He took another step back. His hands literally ached from the need to reach out and touch her once again. Any touch. "I'll be right back."

Becky nodded and slowly eased back into her seat.

The baby had slept all through their meal. At first DJ had been glad for the quiet dinner time. Now he figured having Brittany wake up wouldn't be a bad thing. If Becky continued to stare at him with such wondrous curiosity in her eyes, and with nothing to hold him back—no duty on call, no baby to rock or feed—the few strands of self-control that kept him tethered to reality might just snap.

"Big slice or little slice?" he asked.

"Little. I ate too much." She moved from the table to the sofa.

Shaking his thoughts clear, he grabbed a dish in each hand and crossed into the living room. Time to cool everyone down. "I have a little more data on the mother."

"Really?" She accepted the plate from him.

"Her history certainly explains why she didn't have any qualms leaving a baby with strangers."

She stabbed at the dessert. "Like what?"

"Runaway at sixteen, a few run-ins with the law but no jail time. Married. Divorced. Off the grid until she popped back up in San Diego—"

"Where she met Ethan."

DJ nodded. "It fits."

"But you're not sure?"

"I don't know what I am. One minute I think it makes perfect sense. There are plenty of frog hogs at Miramar looking for a hookup."

"Frog hogs?"

The second the derogatory words were out, he wished he could roll them back in. "That's what the SEALs call the groupies who crave the spotlight of being with a SEAL."

"But Ethan's not a SEAL."

"No, but the pilots get a lot of action just for being around Miramar." And again, open mouth insert foot. Not that it wasn't the truth, and by the accepting look on Becky's face, she already knew it, but still, he felt a strong need to keep her in rose colored glasses when it came to his brother. "Anyhow, the real problem may be in that Ethan has never hid where he's from. Anyone with a computer—"

Becky's fork fell to her plate. "The ranch…"

"The ranch." DJ nodded. Apparently he and his brothers weren't the only one's coming to the conclusion that this whole mess might be nothing more than one big scam. And didn't that just make for a peachy end to another day?

● ● ● ●

Panic and relief warred within Becky and guilt came stumbling in behind them. A sense of relief that Ethan hadn't fathered a child with a weekend hookup lurched inside her only to be tamped down at the idea of little Brittany being nothing more than a pawn in a con. A scam that affected all the Farradays.

Was she a horrible person to hope Brittany wasn't Ethan's child? But if she wasn't a Farraday, then what would happen to Brittany? If the papers the mother had left were nothing more than a scheme to… "Wait a minute. If Brittany's mom relinquished her parental rights and is nowhere to be found, how could she benefit from the ranch?"

"Adam and Brooks and I batted those same questions around this afternoon."

"And?"

"Bottom line is even if Ethan can't keep it in his pants," he paused and she knew he was rethinking his choice of words. His efforts to spare her feelings made her want to smile. "Sorry," he continued, "but when we think of Ethan, hearth and home aren't the first images to pop into mind—"

"More like skydiving and speed racing," she cut in.

"Exactly, but even so, can you see Ethan turning away Brittany's mother if she came to him for help?"

DJ had a point. The guy she'd fallen for in the first grade had a protective streak a mile wide. Which was why Ethan did his flying and racing and other crazy stunts in the military. He could get his adrenaline rush and protect mom's apple pie and the American way all at the same time.

"If she was in trouble and needed a little cash to get by till the next job. Needed a good lawyer to stay out of jail—"

"You think she's that bad?"

He shrugged. "I don't know, but it's a possibility."

"Surely she had to know y'all were going to order DNA testing?"

DJ pinched the bridge of his nose. "Yeah. One would think so. Damn." He dropped his hand and shook his head. "Sorry. Again. Until the DNA results come back, we're just spinning our wheels."

"Agreed." Before Becky could consider what to say next, Brittany let them know she was ready for her next meal. Loudly. "Time to put adult conversation aside."

"I'll get the bottle ready." DJ circled widely around her on his way to the kitchen.

For just a moment Becky hesitated, her gaze on DJ, her mind on the last three days of playing house. She hadn't imagined DJ the domestic type. Rugged, handsome, knight in shining armor material—absolutely, but domestic diva changing diapers, prepping bottles and making dinner—even if it was take out—was so not what she'd expected from him. The Farraday men most definitely did not disappoint, and didn't that send her mind to asking what other hidden talents did Declan James Farraday have?

CHAPTER FIFTEEN

"**H**ey cuz." Ian Farraday strolled through DJ's office door.

No need to ask what brought the Texas Ranger to his office in the middle of a weekday. Popping in from Austin for lunch was not likely. "Long time." Plastering on a sincere smile, DJ stood and met his cousin half way for a back-slapping man hug. "Last time I looked, they don't let family investigate family."

"Nope." Ian slid into the wooden guest chair by DJ's desk. "Though the state stops considering people kin after first cousins, they're still not going to let me take this case."

"Farraday is Farraday." DJ chuckled. Ian was the oldest of Uncle George's grandchildren. Which made DJ and Ian second cousins, not that the Farradays paid attention to degrees. Technically, George Farraday was DJ's great uncle, but as far as everyone was concerned, he was simply Uncle George and Ian was simply a cousin.

"Escorted a witness to Abilene, figured I was so close it would be a sin not to come by and visit in person."

"You mean check up on me?"

Ian shrugged. "You look old enough to take care of yourself."

"Thanks for noticing. So where's your partner? Not traveling in pairs today?" DJ dipped his chin and watched his cousin closely.

"On his way back to Austin. I rented a car." Ian shrugged a lazy shoulder. "I also hear you have a new baby in house."

"Boy, you state boys are getting better at Intel." Even amongst family, the subject of city cop vs state cop was great fodder for a plethora of jokes and jabs he and Ian had been the target of for ages.

"Not that good." Ian laughed. "Mom spoke with Aunt Eileen yesterday."

Smiling, DJ shook his head. "I wonder why she didn't simply post a full page ad in the Austin papers."

Ian waved his hands palms up. "What fun is there in that?"

"I should never have taught her how to use the camera on her computer."

"Look on the bright side, when they're old and senile they can still entertain each other visiting via computer."

"Oh won't that be a laugh a minute." DJ had a hard time thinking of his Aunt Eileen as old and senile. She looked as good today as she did when she'd come to live with them twenty-five years ago. And Ian's mom looked more like Ian's sister than his mother.

"So not going there." Ian smothered a smile and slowly shook his head from side to side.

The two women had been close friends ever since DJ's mom passed. Aunt Anne and his mother had been friends, but Aunt Anne and his Aunt Eileen got along like a house on fire. DJ always thought that not having been born a Farraday gave them strong common roots, but the fact that both were fearless probably had more to do with it.

A knock sounded on the doorframe and Esther filled the space. "Got a call from Mr. Porter. Says a passel of teens are partying in his field again and, I quote, *imbibing copious amounts of hooch.*"

"Interesting word choices." Ian's grin broadened.

"You want me to send someone out there?" Esther asked.

Normally, DJ would have grabbed his hat and driven out to deal with the kids himself, but things weren't going to be normal for a while. "Call Reed. Ask him what he wants to do."

Esther hesitated a long minute, then gave a single curt nod. "This investigating stuff had better get settled soon."

Not till Esther had disappeared from sight did DJ face his cousin. "Any idea when someone will be here?"

"Soon." Ian leaned forward. "They're sending investigators from company B. No connection to the family anywhere near Dallas. Should be here tomorrow or the next day."

DJ nodded. He also was pretty sure with all the state had to deal with if the Texas Rangers were arriving in a day or so, his cousin probably pulled in a favor. Or two. Any officer of the law who had fired a weapon in the line of duty knew what the days ahead were like. The readiness to help a stranger was almost a way of life in this part of the country. But for Farradays, even with the physical distance between the cousins near Austin and the ones firmly planted in West Texas, the willingness to step out on a limb for kin was as key to life and survival as taking a breath. "Thanks."

Ian opened his mouth and raised his hand, ready to disavow his part in moving the investigation to the top of the pile when DJ raised a single brow at him and Ian's hand fell to his side, his mouth snapped shut and his head bobbed. "For the record, I didn't do anything."

DJ just nodded. Off the record was all that really mattered.

Once again Esther appeared at his door. "Check your cell. Someone named Brooklyn says your phone is going straight to voicemail."

"Thanks." He checked his phone. Everything was fine, including the notice of a missed call. "Some days I wonder if there's a leprechaun god of cell phones and if we tick him off, he creates senseless havoc with our reception." The phone in his hand rang and he instantly recognized Brooklyn's number. "Farraday."

"You sound pretty chipper for a guy stuck on desk duty."

Damn this guy was good. "You heard?"

"Your dispatcher told me when I called a few minutes ago looking for you."

"I should have guessed. You calling for a reason or just miss my voice?"

"Don't let my wife hear you talking like that." There was laughter in Brooklyn's tone.

"No problem, you're too tall for me anyhow."

"Got that right." Brooklyn laughed and DJ hoped this meant he was about to receive good news. The only problem was, at this moment, he wasn't so sure what which answer would be good.

"What ya got for me?"

• • • •

Most days the sight of Eileen Callahan and Becky's grandmother strolling through the clinic front door would have been a good thing. Today, she wasn't so sure.

"Oh good," her grandmother said, "you're not busy."

How her grandmother concluded a waiting room filled with people and their pets and a stack of files in her arms meant she wasn't busy made no sense to Becky. "I don't know about that."

"Well, you have to eat." Eileen looked around. "I'm sure you can make time for lunch. You and the baby."

Oh, Eileen Callahan did not do innocent well. Becky didn't know what the woman wanted but undergoing Chinese water torture held more appeal at the moment than winding up in her grandmother and Eileen's crossfire. "Actually, I don't see..."

"Look who woke up." Coming down the hall from the staff room where they kept the bassinet one of the patients had loaned them so Becky wouldn't have to keep packing and unpacking the porta crib, Adam sported a huge grin and carried a tiny baby. "Found her on my way from the exam room gurgling and making the cutest sounds. Do you think she's singing?"

"I wouldn't be surprised." Aunt Eileen held out her arms to receive the bundle. "Grace did that all the time. Always making noise. I couldn't decide if she was talking to herself or humming or what. By the time she was three and wandered about singing her version of opera, we decided all those months as a baby she must have been singing too."

Adam stiffened slightly as he handed off the baby, avoiding his aunt's gaze.

"Oh she is precious." Her grandmother wiggled long polished fingernails in front of the baby grabbing Brittany's attention. "It won't be easy giving this one up when they find her a permanent home."

"Or kin," Eileen added.

Kin? Did Eileen know? Was that why she was here? Oh crap, now Becky seriously would rather undergo water torture.

Adam leaned in and kissed his aunt on the cheek. "I need to take care of Mrs. Peabody's cat."

"Sadie again?" Eileen turned her head looking for the elderly woman.

Adam shook his head. "Sinatra."

Turning to face her nephew, Eileen lowered her voice. "Those poor cats must be sick and tired of getting dragged in here for no good reason."

"Nah, we give extra treats." Adam turned to Becky. "Is Mrs. Peabody in 2 or 3?"

"She's in 2. I'll be right behind you."

Adam nodded, raised a hand holding a file and waved at his aunt. "Catch you later."

At that moment, Kelly leaned over the counter. "Let the doc know that Brooks just called and I reported all was AOK."

"Something wrong?" Aunt Eileen spun about quickly to face Kelly.

"No. He's just checking up on how Brittany's doing with the new formula." Kelly squinted her eyes making funny faces at the baby. "Oh, there go the fingers. Time for lunch."

"Isn't that cute." Becky's grandmother reached to take the child from her friend. "It's been ages since I've fed a little one. Especially one so adorable. Just look how she sucks on those two fingers."

"Yeah, we thought it was rather odd that she sucks her two first fingers not her thumb," Kelly eased back to her seat. "But Brooks said it's not that unusual, Finn and Grace did that too."

"Yes, they did." Aunt Eileen handed the infant over to her friend, studying the baby a little too closely for Becky's comfort, then turned back to Kelly. "When did he say that?"

"One of the times he was here."

"Oh." Aunt Eileen smiled. "He comes by often?"

"Sure." Kelly smiled back. "DJ comes by to visit her too." Kelly tossed her pencil on the table. "Shall I get her bottle ready?"

"Would you mind?" Becky needed to get back to work and send her grandmother on her merry way before DJ's aunt figured out what her nephews were hiding. "Then I can help Doc with the cat."

"You bet." Kelly hurried around the counter and taking Brittany into her arms, lifted the baby's tiny arm and waved it. "Say bye bye to everyone."

"Maybe we can do lunch another day," Becky said, taking one step closer to the exam room where Adam was.

"And since you don't seem to be in any hurry to make me a great-grandmother, we'll do it while you still have the baby," her grandmother said.

Becky nodded. "Sounds like a plan."

"Yes." Aunt Eileen spun around to her friend. "Come on, Dorothy. I've changed my mind about lunch."

The two women marched out of the clinic and Becky had the strangest feeling the world as she knew it was about to be turned on a dime.

CHAPTER SIXTEEN

“The reports just crossed my desk. Sending a paper copy to your house with the results,” Brooklyn explained.

“And…”

“*You* are off the hook.”

DJ’s chest constricted.

“But,” Brooklyn continued, “it’s still a match.”

“Ethan,” he whispered then noticed Ian’s eyes widening and realized his cousin must be thinking something had happened to Ethan overseas. Shaking his head, DJ waved off Ian’s concerns with his free hand.

“Whoever papa is,” Brooklyn continued, “they’re a very close relative of yours.”

“So she’s a Farraday.” Air filled his lungs again. Now he knew what good news looked like.

“Yep. That’s why I didn’t want this send these results via hackable channels.”

“Appreciate that.” A smile teased the corners of his mouth. He was pleased. And the way Ian’s brows rose high on his forehead the poor guy was confused. An expressive Farraday trait all the cousins had in common. “Now all I have to do is get a hold of Ethan.”

“Still no word?” Brooklyn’s tone softened.

DJ shook his head. “No. But he can’t stay offline forever.”

“Hmm,” Brooklyn grunted. They both knew anything was possible in this crazy war that supposedly wasn’t a war anymore. “Let me see if I can’t get some info.”

“Yeah. Thanks. I’m going to have to get word to him. Decisions have to be made and Ethan’s the one to make them.”

"Understood," Brooklyn said quickly. "Will let you know as soon as I hear anything more."

"Sounds good. I know I keep saying this, but thanks." DJ disconnected the call and stared at his phone, sorting through the conversation. Brooklyn understood as well as he did the possibilities for why Ethan wasn't responding. If he was busy as hell flying day and night, going long stretches without checking in wasn't uncommon, but this many days was pushing it. DJ was rooting for special training that for whatever reason required limited communication. Isolation during some training programs wasn't uncommon. And the safest scenario. The last option was the one that concerned everyone. Total communication blackout due to something very classified. And probably very dangerous.

"So did that sound the way I think it did?"

"Maybe." DJ tossed his phone on the desk. "The abandoned baby is Ethan's."

"You're sure?"

"Well, we're sure she's mom's granddaughter and she's not my daughter, and Adam, Brooks, Connor and Finn haven't been anywhere near California so that leaves…"

"Ethan." Ian sat back. "Well, life with you guys is never boring."

"No. Not these days."

"What happens now?"

"For a start, I need to pull Brittany out of the system."

"You got anything more than the word of whomever you just spoke to?"

DJ nodded and explained all that had gone down in the last few days from the disappearing dog to the childhood friend with a brain tumor to his buddy the former Navy SEAL.

"Damn. You guys do keep life interesting."

DJ pushed to his feet. "You got enough time to stick around for supper at the ranch? Aunt Eileen will be pissed if she doesn't see you. And with this late breaking news, everyone will be there."

"Damn right they will." Eileen walked into DJ's office and closed the door behind her.

"Where's Dorothy?" DJ asked, hoping to give the fire in Aunt Eileen's gaze time to simmer down. "Thought you were having lunch in town today."

"Dropped her off at the café. She and the girls are starting without me."

Ian came to his feet to greet his aunt. "Still playing cards?"

"Sorry, handsome. Good to see you." Though she wasn't technically his aunt at all, all the cousins had called her Aunt Eileen just the same, and she treated them all as her own. The arms that wrapped around Ian were no exception. "You go ahead and take your seat. I just need a minute here."

Ian looked from Aunt Eileen to DJ and bit back a chuckle. "Better you than me."

DJ opened his mouth to speak when Aunt Eileen's hands rose up and dropped at her waist. "Your brothers spent so much time on the back porch last night smoking cigars I'm surprise they didn't wake up with black lung."

"I'll—" DJ started.

Aunt Eileen's one hand shot up, shaking a finger at him. "Y'all are hiding something from me and I want to know right now what it is."

"Well—"

"Don't *well* me. It's that baby, isn't it?"

"I was—"

"She hums like Grace. She sucks on her two fingers like Adam, Finn and Grace. Y'all are hovering over that baby, especially you at Becky's every night since the infant arrived. That little bundle's got that same button face all you kids had." Aunt Eileen's hands landed flat on his desk. "Declan James Farraday, is that your baby?"

• • • •

Mrs. Peabody's cat, named for the famous crooner, was overweight, mellow, and probably a bit on the arthritic side, but most definitely did not need a visit to the vet's office. Still, Adam offered the appropriate *hmm* and grunt to make Nadine Peabody feel she'd had good cause to bring the animal in. Adam gave her some liquid *medicine* to give the kitty twice a day, vitamins actually, but what the old woman didn't know wouldn't hurt her. Adam had been giving the old cat placebos for years to keep the lonely patient happy.

Becky wished the same were true of the next pet. Poor pup was riddled with cancer and she could tell by the way Adam tightened his lips that the prognosis was not good.

A rap came from the door and Kelly popped her head inside. "Sorry to interrupt, but you're needed outside, Beck."

"Not my aunt again?" Adam asked.

"No." Kelly shook her head, glanced at the pup and his owner, and then tipped her head toward the hall.

"Go on." Adam urged Becky forward with a lift of his chin. "I can handle this on my own."

Becky peeled off the rubber gloves, tossed them in the trash and, once out in the hall, pulled the exam room door shut behind her, bumping into Kelly. "Ouch. Why are you stopping?"

"I wanted to give you a heads up," Kelly whispered.

"Heads up?"

"There's a woman in the break room with Brittany waiting for you."

"What woman?" Becky turned to where the baby stayed in her bassinet.

Kelly grabbed her arm. "Becky, she's from Protective Services."

Becky balked, looking up the hall then back to the door she'd just come out of. "I'd better call DJ."

"I already did. Left a voice mail."

"Okay," Becky sighed, "but he has to be at the station, he's on desk duty. I'll go talk to the lady and you give Esther a call. Have her give him a message to call me right away. Better yet, have him get his backside over here ASAP. As soon as Adam is through, let him know where I am also." She knew there would be a home visit to deal with, but somehow she'd not expected it to be so soon. For some reason, even though this was strictly routine, facing the woman alone scared her. Lord how she wished DJ would waltz through the door.

• • • •

Some days it didn't pay to get out of bed. DJ met his aunt's angry gaze. "No."

Aunt Eileen retreated a step. Confusion softened her piercing glare. "Then who?"

"Ethan," DJ said softly.

Stumbling back, she landed in the chair beside Ian. "Ethan?"

DJ nodded.

"Does he know?"

"I only just found out myself a few minutes ago."

"And you're sure?"

Both Ian and DJ nodded.

Aunt Eileen looked from man to man and then a shaky smile slowly grew stronger. "I'm finally a grandmother."

• • • •

"Knock knock," Becky said as she tapped lightly on the open door. "I'm Rebecca Wilson."

"Oh, hello." The middle aged woman with shoulder length black hair and strong lines on her face that reminded others what a tough job she had, backed away from the bassinet and shot her arm out at Becky. "I'm Missy Baxter."

Becky shook the proffered hand, then felt the need to connect with Brittany. Already awake and doing that babbly-humming sound, Brittany happily ignored the adults in the room. As soon as

Becky picked her up, as Brittany had done on a regular basis over the last few days, she'd immediately curled into Becky's shoulder.

The woman focused on Brittany. "Looks like you've bonded."

What was the right answer? Yes? No? A little? Becky settled for a smile.

Missy opened a solitary folder on the nearby table. "When you were certified for emergency foster care, you lived elsewhere?"

"That's right." Becky rocked in place, patting Brittany's back.

"I'm a bit confused as to your current address. I thought I was coming to your home."

"It's upstairs."

"Excuse me?"

"I live in the apartment over the clinic."

"Oh." A thin line deepened between the social worker's brow.

That unsettling sensation that had taken root in the pit of Becky's stomach at the news protective services was here to speak with her took an instant dive in the direction of serious trouble warning system. "It's a very nice apartment. Would you like to see it?"

She closed the folder. "Well, actually—"

Adam walked into the room directly toward Miss Baxter and cut off the conversation. "How do you do? I'm Adam Farraday."

"That's right." The woman smiled and extended her hand. "You're the police chief's brother."

"One of them." Adam flashed a high watt smile. "I just put in a call to his office. He should be here shortly."

"Oh, that will save me a trip. He was my next stop."

"Really?" Becky eked out.

"Yes. You see I wanted to come to you first to explain—"

Clattering heels thundering loudly outside the door came to an abrupt halt as Toni blew into the room. "I was across the street delivering more cakeballs when Brooks told me Protective Services is here."

"Brooks?" Becky mumbled. "How did—"

"I called him too," Adam explained.

Becky nodded. "I see."

Missy Baxter stared at Toni. "I'm afraid I don't."

"Oh, so sorry. I'm Antoinette Farraday."

"Another Farraday." Miss Baxter seemed to be processing the information.

"My husband is Brooks," Toni filled in.

"The doctor," Becky added at the woman's perplexed expression.

Missy Baxter nodded as Meg came barreling through the doorway. "Am I too late?"

"For what?" Becky asked.

Meg shrugged. "I don't know, but where I come from whenever a government agency is involved in anything, it usually means trouble."

"Oh I can assure you—" Missy started, shaking her head.

Brooks practically flew from the hall into the tiny break room, and didn't stop until he stood beside his bride, wrapping his arm firmly around Toni's waist. "Left everyone sitting at the office, so hopefully this won't take long." He looked at the only new face in the room. "You must be –"

"Missy Baxter, protective services." She accepted Brooks' proffered hand with a tired smile.

"Nice to meet you." Meg extended her hand to the woman as well and with her other hand jerked a thumb in Adam's direction then tucked herself into his side. "I'm married to this guy."

Right about now with Brooks and Toni and Adam and Meg paired off, standing side by side to face down the person who would decide if Brittany stayed or went, and *if* Brittany had to go, would decide who she'd go with, Becky really wished DJ were here with her too.

"I think there must be some mis—" Missy started to speak again.

"No one is laying one finger on my grandchild." Aunt Eileen stood in the doorway, legs askance, hands on her hips with DJ closing in on her heels and her nephew Ian beside him.

"Hi, Missy," DJ shimmied around his aunt and shot his hand out. "Didn't expect to see you here quite so soon."

"Yes, well," her gaze darting from one side of the room to the other, Missy offered a shaky smile, "I didn't expect such a, uh, large welcoming committee."

DJ glanced at most of his family standing to one side of the room behind Becky and across from Missy Baxter. The poor woman looked like the lone prisoner in front of a firing squad. "Neither did I."

"No one is taking this baby anywhere," Aunt Eileen repeated.

"And you are?" Missy asked.

"Eileen Callahan." The stern expression showed his aunt wasn't used to people not knowing who she was. Most anyone raised in the county knew each other and few people didn't know the Farraday name. Missy had only moved to the area little over a year ago.

If not for an incident late last year when a drunk driver made the mistake of speeding through Tuckers Bluff with her two children in the backseat and sufficient marijuana stashed in the trunk to supply the entire state, DJ wouldn't have known Missy either. "I was just going to give your office a call," he said.

"I was about to explain to Miss Wilson that we had some movement in the system and a permanent foster home has opened up for Brittany in Butler Springs—"

A deafening cascade of voices erupted.

Aunt Eileen's being the loudest. Her, "That will not be necessary," was almost drowned out by Meg's question, "What does it take to become a permanent foster parent?" and Toni chimed in with a different tack, "Does it help to be a medical professional?"

"Yes. Of course." Brooks smiled down at his wife. On an adoration scale the two were off the charts.

"We can too," Meg volunteered this time.

The clamoring of voices, one over the other as each member of DJ's family insisted they could take care of Brittany even though no one knew yet about the DNA results, was almost deafening. Even though Aunt Eileen knew for sure the baby was a Farraday, DJ had no doubt that she would have been just as insistent no matter what.

"What about me?" Becky shouted silencing the others. She kissed the top of Brittany's head. "Why can't I keep her?"

"That's what I was getting to." Missy paused to scan the room before settling her gaze back on Becky. DJ got the feeling the social worker expected to be interrupted. When no one attempted to speak, she continued, "We do have a foster care family ready to take Brittany on, but if you'd like to keep her, Miss Wilson, you have the option of changing your status."

Becky shifted Brittany to her other shoulder and took a step closer to the social worker. Holding her chin high, she tightened her hold on the baby. "I'll do it."

CHAPTER SEVENTEEN

"Time out." DJ positioned himself beside Becky and in front of Missy.

Becky's gut clenched. What news was coming down now? When the social worker had announced she'd be taking Brittany away, Becky panicked. The words "I'll do it" had come out of her mouth before she'd had the chance to think it through. And that was just fine. At this point she didn't care who Brittany's father was. There was no way she was letting this precious child into the foster care system. She might have to move back with her grandmother, but she would find a way to make this work.

"There's additional information." DJ held out a few sheets of paper. "These are copies of Brittany's birth certificate and release of parental rights."

"Really?" Heavy undertones of irritation laced Missy's response. Becky hadn't realized that DJ had withheld that information from the state.

"Brittany has immediate family here in Tuckers Bluff," DJ continued.

Flipping pages, Missy studied the papers thoroughly before flipping back and starting again.

DJ inched closer to Becky but continued to address the social worker. "I should have corroborating DNA results sometime today or tomorrow."

Both Adam and Brooks swung their gazes in DJ's direction. Becky knew what they were asking. The same thing everyone wanted to know. A single drop of DJ's chin answered their silent question. Yes, the DNA results were back and Brittany is definitely a Farraday. Becky should have been elated at the news.

As soon as the family was able to reach Ethan, he should be coming home. And if he was half the man she still believed him to be, he'd be staying home as soon as the Marine Corps allowed. So why wasn't she ready to dance for joy? A real chance to get Ethan to notice her as a wife, mother, lifetime companion and not as just the skinny kid always under foot alongside his little sister.

"Why," the social worker looked up at DJ, "weren't we given these before?"

DJ blew out the tiniest of sighs that Becky had come to recognize as his raising his guard. "There were doubts of the veracity of the data."

"But not anymore?" Her voice harsher, gritty, she looked from brother to brother. "Which one of you is Ethan?"

"He's not here," DJ answered, his stance stiffer. "Active duty marine. I apologize—"

Missy held up her hand and shook her head. "Save it. In spite of the fact that I have a stack of files up to my nose on my desk and could have been using my time more wisely on any one of those cases, I am glad to have one less child in the system. What I am most definitely not thrilled with is the way this entire matter has been handled." She held up the papers she'd just read and some of the tension in her features seemed to soften. "May I keep these?"

"Yes. That's your copy." DJ's stance relaxed a fraction.

"Very well." Lifting a briefcase from the floor she set it on a nearby table, opened it, slid the folder and new papers inside, and then closing it, quickly scanned the assembled group of people silently staring as though waiting for her to perform a new circus trick. "There's still some paperwork to be done, but I'll let y'all work out who actually cares for Brittany on your own."

DJ relaxed a bit more and his arm brushed against Becky's. Leaning closer in her direction, his warmth, his mere presence gave her strength and courage, and at the same time shoved her heart down a steep slide to the pit of her stomach. The family would be making new arrangements now. DJ wouldn't need her.

Wouldn't smile at her like she'd hung the moon for making him coffee in the morning. Wouldn't look at her as though she were the top contender in a beauty pageant. Wouldn't be sleeping on the other side of the bed, fully clothed, on top of the covers to preserve her honor and keep her from sleeping on the sofa. Even if at her size it did make more sense.

Looking at him, she blinked to hide the tears pushing to the surface. No more silly conversations with the lighter side of the big bad police officer. No more butterflies in her stomach every time he came near. No more warm and fuzzy feelings when he played with the baby. No more DJ.

Her breath caught and her heart flapped around like a landed trout struggling to breathe. *Oh my lord*. Becky's jaw snapped shut. She was in love—honest to God real love—with Declan James Farraday. *Holy crap*. What the heck was she supposed to do now?

• • • •

DJ held his breath. He'd taken a hell of a risk withholding the papers with Ethan's name on it and only sharing the personal letter with the mother's name. He'd hoped to have confirmation before Missy had moved along so far as the home visit.

He followed the social worker to the front of the clinic and out the door. At her car, as was expected of every good Texas born and bred boy, he'd opened her door for her.

Missy tossed her briefcase onto the passenger side and with one hand on the top of the door spun around to face him. "I really am glad this is going to work out without putting the baby in the system."

"I sense a *but* coming." He tried for an easy smile, but with tension coursing through him so thick and strong he suspected his grin may have looked more like a nervous twitch.

"For the record," she paused for him to nod, "pull a stunt like that again and I'll see you in court and you'll be the one needing a star witness."

DJ bobbed his head. "Understood."

He remained rooted to the sidewalk as Missy's car drove away, a headache building between his temples. "Damn it, Ethan, where are you?"

Tapping at his phone, DJ flipped to Facebook first. Nothing new posted by his brother. Even knowing it was a waste of time he sent another message: NEED TO TALK ASAP. IMPORTANT. STAY SAFE. DJ had lost count of the number of messages sent and not responded to. The rest of his brothers had done the same. Texts, messages, computer calls and emails all unanswered. At least now they knew for sure about the baby.

Ian appeared beside him, slipping his phone into his pocket. "Going to have to pass on the dinner invitation after all."

"Duty calls?"

"'Fraid so." Ian hesitated. "Listen, I may be overstepping my bounds here."

"Never." DJ smiled and slapped his cousin on the back.

"Good, 'cause I don't know when I'll be back this way. About you and Becky—"

"There is no me and Becky." DJ took a half step back. "And speaking of Becky, I'd better get back inside."

Ian grabbed hold of DJ's arm as he spun away. "I disagree. Everyone in there was watching that woman and the baby."

"And?"

"I watched you." Ian let go of his arm. "Watching Becky."

"I wasn't—"

"Yes. You were. Every time the mention of papers came up your gaze drifted to see how Becky took the information. Every time that protective services woman opened her mouth you inched a fraction closer to Becky. You couldn't have been more territorial if you'd peed on her leg."

"That's—"

"And she's in just as deep."

"Now I know you're crazy. She loves Ethan. Always has."

"Maybe, but she's *in* love with you." Ian waited a moment for some response then shook his head. "Okay. Don't listen to me. But when you go back inside, pay attention man. Just pay attention." Ian jingled his keys in his hand and crossed the street to where he'd parked his rental car.

Pay attention. DJ spun back around and yanked at the front door. What the hell else did Ian think he'd been doing for days? He'd noticed all sorts of things about Becky he shouldn't have noticed. How the sunlight bounced off her hair. The twinkle in her eyes every time she smiled. The gentle rise and fall of her chest under the blankets when she'd finally drifted soundly to sleep. The easy way Brittany snuggled into her shoulder. The feeling of coming home, not to a place but to her. How delicious his morning coffee tasted when she made it, or how wonderful she smelled after a shower, after work, and after the baby spit up on her. *Damn.*

He'd barely made it down the hall when half the Farraday clan filed out of the staff room, Aunt Eileen leading the pack. "Where's everyone going?" he asked.

"The baby has a routine." Aunt Eileen came to a stop in front of him, a broad smile on her face.

"And I have to get back to the office." Brooks kissed his wife on the nose. "You going to be all right?"

"I am." Toni smiled up at her husband as he scooted around his aunt and past DJ.

Meg squeezed Adam's hand. "And I'd better let you get back to your patients."

Adam's gaze shot over her head to the few people and their pets patiently waiting to be seen. "Yeah."

Down the hall, Becky came slowly out of the break room and stopped by the doorway. Worried eyes locked with his and he had to tamp down the urge to push his family aside and rush to reassure her everything would be just fine. And wasn't Ian right about that too. Pissing on her leg indeed.

"Dorothy and Ruth Ann are probably almost finished with lunch by now," Aunt Eileen continued. "You and Becky have everything under control." Aunt Eileen shook her head and gave up an amused chuckle. "That girl is so much like her grandmother. Adam and Brooks make sense. Though you shouldn't have kept this from Sean and me, for now it's best to wait and speak with Ethan before we make any more decisions."

DJ was baffled by how the woman who had been spitting mad that no one was taking her grandbaby away from her could be calm and downright cheery. Even if Brittany was technically a great-niece, the message was clearly understood. So what the heck did he miss by stepping outside? His aunt pushed up onto her tippy toes and gave him a kiss on the cheek. "Call if you need anything."

The corridor clear of all his family except Adam, DJ glanced back to Becky making her way up the hall.

"I told Becky she could have the afternoon off if she wanted," Adam said. "But she insists on staying and working."

"She can be pretty stubborn when she wants." His mind drifted back to the first night at her place and the battle of the bed. He'd wanted to stay on the couch for a lot of reasons and in the end, she'd gotten her way and he'd shared the bed with her. Sort of.

Adam grabbed a folder and walked away. DJ couldn't bring his feet to move. He had to be out of his mind dragging this out. Totally, one hundred percent, batshit crazy. Both of his sisters-in-law and his Aunt had been willing to take over caring for Brittany. Too bad he wasn't ready to give up the job. Or Becky.

"I guess deep down we knew it was true." Becky came to a stop beside him.

DJ hefted one shoulder. "You might have been sure, but the rest of us not so much."

"Brittany's asleep again and I have to get back to work."

"Go." DJ let his hand land on her arm and instantly regretted the simple motion. There was nothing simple about the affect she had on him. "I'm going to take a minute with my niece before I head back to the station."

Becky smiled sweetly and he noticed this time the sparkle didn't reach her eyes. And that didn't sit well with him either. Blast.

In a few long strides, he was in the small room that felt palatial without all the people, and stood at his niece's crib side. His niece. That's twice he'd said it and the words still sounded so strange to his ears. His cell phone sounded off. Swiping at the phone, he put it to his ear. "Farraday."

"Declan, man. How's it going?"

"The same as it was an hour ago when we hung up. What's up?" A big part of him didn't want Brooklyn to answer. Something about no-news-is-good-news.

"I haven't been able to confirm which team is involved."

Already those few words had icy fingers tracing up his spine.

"There's no easy way to say this. A helo went down…"

CHAPTER EIGHTEEN

"Well, it's about time you showed up." Dorothy handed Eileen some rolled up silverware.

"It couldn't be helped." Eileen unwrapped the napkin, dumping a knife and fork on the table. "But this is so much better than we'd imagined. Well, most of it."

"Most of it?" Ruth Ann asked. There wasn't any poker game this afternoon, just an impromptu lunch after Eileen and Dorothy had joined forces on a fact-finding mission.

"Did you fill her in?" Eileen asked.

Dorothy shook her head. "Only that you didn't like the way the boys smoked cigars all night and were sure my Becky had answers for you."

"And she did."

Halfway through her dessert, Dorothy put her fork down on the plate. "What answers? She barely said a word."

"Ever since the day that baby arrived in town I knew something was fishy. I just didn't realize how fishy."

"I still don't." Ruth Ann took a bite of Frank's pecan pie and Eileen quickly recapped her suspicions, her awkward accusation of DJ and the final unveiling of who Brittany belonged to. Ruth leaned back, her pie forgotten. "Oh, wow. I didn't see that coming."

"There's more." Eileen's smile pulled at her cheeks.

"How much more can there be?" Dorothy reached for her glass of water.

"You and I are finally going to be real kin."

Dorothy's glass froze half way to her mouth. "Is Ethan coming home?"

"I have no earthly idea. I don't pay attention to his coming and goings. Makes me less nervous if I just picture him all the time at the camp pub."

"Pub, in the Middle East?" Ruth Ann muttered before shaking her head. "Sorry."

"So explain." Dorothy pushed her plate away. "How are we going to become kin?"

"Becky and DJ." Eileen rubbed her hands together enthusiastically.

Dorothy glared at her longtime friend. "Are you mad?"

"Don't you see?" Eileen leaned forward. "Think about it. How did all this start?"

When Dorothy said nothing Ruth Ann volunteered, "Someone left a baby at the station,"

"Actually," Dorothy paused, her brows creased in thought, "DJ called Becky over the dog."

"See!" Eileen sat back, excitement bubbling inside her. Feast or famine. One day a bunch of bachelors with no next generation babies in sight and now two married men, one more well on his way, and DJ falling fast with a plethora of the next generation about. "And we don't have to do a thing."

"No. I don't see." Ruth Ann seemed to be losing brain cells with each new gray hair, or maybe her ponytail was too tight.

"The dog showed up on the stationhouse door." Eileen enunciated clearly. "DJ called Becky over the dog."

"Oh my God." Dorothy smiled. "The dog brought them together."

"Yep." Eileen crossed her arms and nodded. "Now we just have to let them, and the baby, work things out."

Ruth Ann shook her head. "I think y'all are crazy expecting a dog to play matchmaker."

"We'll see." Eileen smiled. "We'll see."

• • • •

All the color drained from DJ's face and Becky knew whatever he'd been told it had to do with Ethan. She'd seen DJ deal with Meg's crazy former fiancé, Toni's abusive husband and mentally struggle with the Jake Thomas situation. Right now, DJ was rattled and that was a new sight for Becky.

Whatever the person on the other end had said, DJ bobbed his head in response and Becky mouthed *Ethan* to him. When his eyes closed and his chin dropped in a single curt motion, she wished to God Ethan had grown up loving cattle and horses like Connor and Finn. Without giving it any thought, her hand slipped into DJ's and she squeezed, surprised at the comfort coursing through her when he squeezed back.

Standing in the hall was no way to find out what was going on. She turned to face the front desk, caught Kelly's attention and whispered, "We'll be in Adam's office. Send him in when he's done."

Kelly nodded and Becky tugged DJ into the room and closed the door behind them.

"I see," DJ said. "Right." Some color seemed to return to his face.

She couldn't determine how bad any of it was. Though rattled, DJ was still one of the strongest men she knew. A bloody Rock of Gibraltar. Nothing in his stance gave her any hint to what was going on.

"Thanks. Let me know if you hear anything else." The phone beeped and DJ slipped it into his pocket.

"Are you okay?" she asked him softly, her hand still in his.

Eyes filled with tenderness and concern studied her. A fist tightened around her heart, convinced he was going to tell her Ethan was gone. At the same moment, her heart beat stronger at the realization that all the sadness in his gaze seemed directed at her.

"There may be a situation," he said.

Wanting to give him a big old-fashioned comforting hug, she inched forward slightly, not daring to actually wrap her arms around him. "You know whatever it is, I'm here for you. All of you."

DJ blinked and narrow eyes focused on hers. For a second she wondered if he wasn't trying to read her mind. "You really are amazing."

It was her turn to blink with surprise. "Thank you."

"My brother is an idiot."

"Excuse me?"

"Sorry. I shouldn't have said anything, it's just..." He blew out a sigh and lifted his gaze to some distant point over her shoulder and back. "We were right. Ethan was the ride on a recent mission."

She swallowed the words on the tip of her tongue and waited for DJ to finish.

"Nothing is confirmed. All Brooklyn knows is a helo went down. We have no way of confirming if it was Ethan's, but since he's not in touch, we can safely presume it's his."

Her breath caught in her throat as she waited for more.

"The only thing we know is all souls are accounted for."

"Souls? Meaning they're all alive?"

DJ nodded. "From what little Brooklyn's source could tell him, there are injuries. No word that any are life threatening. And we have no idea if Ethan is among them."

"Why don't we know more? Why won't his superiors tell you more?" As much as she wanted to be sure Ethan was all right, she hated his siblings not knowing. His father. "Oh God, Aunt Eileen."

"We probably won't tell her until we know for sure." Once again his gaze searched her eyes with a curious intensity that made her want to shift her weight, but at the same time, like gravitational pull, his eyes kept her rooted in place.

"What?" she asked softly.

"I thought you'd be more upset."

"You said he's alive right?"

DJ nodded.

"Whether he's injured or not, Aunt Eileen is going to freak."

"You're more worried about her than yourself?"

"And you." The words came out very softly. Once she heard herself, she quickly added, "And your brothers and Grace, of course."

Slowly, DJ lifted his thumb and brushed the roughened pad across her bottom lip. The gentle touch sent a zap of electricity all the way to her toes. Balance wasn't an option, she was pretty sure she swayed back, or forward. She wasn't sure. All she knew was his free hand skimmed down her cheek and slipping around her neck, held her steady.

"Rebecca," he said so softly she wasn't completely sure she hadn't imagined hearing her name.

"Uh huh," she mumbled.

"Do you mind if I kiss you?"

"Uh uh," she managed to mutter a second before his mouth came down on hers. The tenderness in the careful touch shattered the tension inside her. Sparks and heat spread like a lit match on dry kindling. All with a sweet, gentle, barely there kiss that ended all too soon.

The warmth of DJ's breath fanned her face, and she sucked in a deep calming breath. Not that it was doing any good. Her heart raced, her blood was pumping and she wanted very much to pull him in for another longer, deeper and delicious kiss.

"About Ethan." DJ pulled back to look at her. "Though technically the family of an injured marine should be notified within twenty-four hours, in reality there's no telling how long it will be before Dad is officially notified of Ethan's status. If he's hurt and what he'll want to do."

"If he's hurt. Bad." She almost choked on her own words. "Are you still going to tell him right away about Brittany?"

DJ hesitated, then shook his head. "I don't know. I honestly don't know."

Becky nodded. She had to think of Ethan as perfectly okay. For everyone's sake, she had to. "While you were outside with Ms. Baxter, Aunt Eileen wanted to take Brittany to the ranch." DJ opened his mouth to speak, and she held up a hand. "Adam suggested it was better for Brittany to stay with a routine she's growing used to. Brooks concurred if it was okay with me."

"Is it? Okay with you?"

Again, Becky bobbed her head. "But I'll still need help."

A smile lifted at one side of his mouth. "I think something can be arranged."

"I was hoping you would say that." She was hoping he'd say a lot more. Do more. Then again, every once in a while a girl had to stand up for herself. Pushing up on her toes and winding both arms around his neck, she didn't give him any time to consider. She tugged his head toward hers and this time threw tender and delicate to the wind.

DJ didn't hesitate in his response. For as many days as they'd been thrown together, he'd been fighting the need to do just this, hold Becky in his arms, see firsthand if she tasted as sweet as he thought. He didn't care about old history. About who she loved as a child. All he cared about was the passion and fire passing between them. Winding an arm around her waist, he pulled her in closer. He needed to feel every slender curve against him the way he needed air to breathe.

"What's so all fired…ookaay." Adam stopped in his tracks and cleared his throat. Twice.

When DJ broke away from Becky, his brother was rubbing his brows, staring at the floor and smiling.

Taking a step back, DJ held onto Becky with one hand, and turned to face his brother. "I have news."

"Yeah. I can see that." Adam looked up, his smile broader. "Shall I call Aunt Eileen?"

"No!" DJ and Becky echoed.

The smile slipped from Adam's face. "What's the news?"

DJ couldn't bring himself to let go of Becky's hand. Now that he'd felt her warmth against him, he couldn't stand to lose the connection. "Ethan's helo went down during a mission. We believe the team made it safely out, but there are injuries."

"Ethan?"

"We don't know. But it doesn't appear any of the injuries are life threatening."

"And you know this how?" Adam asked.

"Brooklyn."

"I need to meet this guy someday." Adam spun around, his hand roughly rubbing the back of his neck. "We can't tell Aunt Eileen. Not yet."

"Agreed," DJ said quickly.

"But Dad needs to know."

"Also agreed."

Becky shook her head. "Don't we get to tell the poor lady anything? She's a pretty strong woman. I think she can take it."

Adam and DJ stared at her.

"What? I'd want that woman in my corner any day."

DJ shifted his attention to his brother. Adam shrugged and waved his hands. "Family meeting. Let Dad decide."

DJ nodded. "Where?"

"We can't do the ranch, or Aunt Eileen will figure it out for sure," Adam said. "We could use our place but then you'd both have to bring the baby."

"I don't have to—" Becky started.

"Yes." DJ squeezed the hand he still held. "You're the smart one today." His lips came down on her temple and even though they were all worried about Ethan, making this connection with Becky had him grinning from the inside out.

"Can we meet at your place?" Adam asked Becky.

Smiling up at DJ, she dragged her gaze away and nodded at Adam. "Sure."

Now the only thing DJ had to work out was how to get through the rest of the day without letting go of Becky.

CHAPTER NINETEEN

L ike it or not, DJ couldn't spend the entire afternoon holding hands with Becky. They both had work to do. Instead, he spent the remainder of the day grinning like a teen after his first slide into second base.

No matter who cared for the baby until Ethan could come home or what arrangements were made for the future, Brittany would need more than a portable crib and carrier. DJ wasn't going to go crazy buying out Sisters, especially since he suspected his aunt would want that pleasure, but that first day shopping, Becky had returned more than once to look at the bouncy thing for babies to sit in. Tonight, he'd decided a few minutes detour to pick it up was in order.

With every step up to Becky's apartment, trepidation and anticipation battled each other deep in his gut. In only a few hours, his entire world had just turned on a dime. This morning he was convinced the nicest girl he knew was in love with his younger brother, he was unsure if he had a niece, and he hadn't a clue if his brother was alive or dead. Now, DJ knew his brother was alive, he had a niece, Becky—Rebecca—Wilson was most definitely not in love with his brother, and if this afternoon was any sign, he just might have a shot at the happiness his older brothers had recently found.

Through the front door at the top of the stairs, he could hear Becky singing. He liked the sound and how it made him feel. As a matter of fact, despite all the crazy crap that had gone down over the last few days, he'd looked forward every night to coming home to Becky. Coming home. He really liked the sound of that. "Patience Romeo," he whispered out loud and pushed open the front door.

"Hey." Becky spun around, waving a wooden spoon. "Since Toni was nice enough to bring pizza last time, I thought I could do spaghetti tonight. Your family should be here any minute."

And why did that let all the air out of his tires. He'd been looking forward to a chance to visit alone. To test the waters so to speak. See where things were going to go after this afternoon's kiss. He'd tried not to dwell on it too much, but from the second he'd parked out front, pulling her into his arms for a big sloppy kiss was front and center on his mind.

"Oh, my." Her gaze fell on the large plastic bag at his side. "What's that?"

Setting the package on the kitchen table, he slid the baby bouncer out for her to see.

Turning off the burner, Becky set the spoon down and glided the short distance to the table. "You didn't."

"I did." For a split second he thought perhaps he'd done the wrong thing. Until she spun around and threw her arms around his neck.

"You, Mr. Declan James Farraday, are one hell of a nice guy."

"Think so?" He tried to hold back the huge grin threatening to spread across his face.

Blushing, she nodded and stepped back.

Instantly, DJ wished he'd trapped her in his arms, but he had to be patient. Just because he already knew she was the one for him didn't mean he didn't have to be careful not to push too hard too soon. *Patience Romeo.* "Are you busy Friday night?"

"No."

First step, hopefully hadn't gotten everything wrong. "Would you like to join me for dinner?"

"That would be nice."

Elation shot up inside him. "I'm sure one of my brothers would be willing to babysit."

A slow, easy smile settled at her lips. "Don't we sound like the old married couple?" Instantly, her eyes rounded and both her hands slapped over her mouth as she mumbled, "Oh my God," and took a step back.

"Hey." He stepped forward reaching out to her.

Taking another step back and squeezing her eyes shut for a long few seconds, she shook her head. "I'm sorry I didn't mean to sound...to imply... I mean." Her hands fell by her side. "I'd better check the sauce."

"Hang on." DJ curled a hand around her elbow as she walked past him and swung her around in front of him. "Please don't run away from me."

"I wasn't running, I need to..." Her gaze darted up to meet his and she blew out a sigh. "Sorry."

"Why?"

"Why?" she repeated.

"Yes. Why are you running away from me?" He seriously didn't understand what just happened. Everything seemed perfectly normal. Nice even. No awkward transitions from this afternoon's really amazing kiss to another night sharing custody of Brittany. What Becky just said was true. They did behave like an old married couple. They'd fallen into a routine with the ease of two people meant to be together. He knew that. Or was that the problem? "Scrap that. New question. Is the idea of being married to a man like me so awful?"

"Oh, God no." Imploring eyes looked up at him. "It's just that..." She sighed again. "I've already made a fool of myself in front of this town. I'd rather not do it again."

"Fool? How?"

"That stupid one-sided schoolgirl crush on Ethan. I don't need the whole town talking about me again." Her gaze darted away from his.

Schoolgirl crush. *Again*. When it came to understanding feminine logic, DJ wasn't much better than any other guy, but right now the picture was beginning to come into focus. A light bulb suddenly brightened over his head. "Wait. Do you mean us?"

Becky nodded.

"The town thinking you have a stupid one-sided schoolgirl crush on me?"

Closing her eyes, she nodded again.

DJ placed a finger under her chin and raised her face. "Look at me."

Her eyes popped open.

"If this afternoon wasn't already perfectly clear, allow me to elaborate. I do not go around kissing women just for the hell of it. If the town is going to say anyone has a silly one-sided crush, it's going to be me."

"You?" Becky's mouth didn't quite close, making him want to kiss away her surprise. "But…"

He put a finger over her lips. "And I'd very much like a chance to see if it can become two-sided."

Wrapping her fingers around his wrist, she shook her head. "Aren't we the pair? Declan James Farraday, it already is two-sided."

A smile pulled at his cheeks. "I like the way you say that."

"It's a beautiful name."

"No," he kissed the tip of her nose, "the two-sided part."

"Oh, that." She smiled up at him. "So what do we do now?"

"We take care of Brittany until her father comes home and when he does, if you don't want to string me up for leaving my dirty socks on the bathroom floor, maybe we can revisit that old married couple thing."

"I like the sound of that already."

He wasn't sure whose arms wound around the other first, but pulling her tightly against him, he poured all the emotion and promise into the kiss. Everything about her was so right. The feel of her hair in his fingers, her lips on his, her delicate curves against his hard planes. So perfect.

Footsteps pounding nearby came to a halt, followed by a loud, course, clearing of a man's throat. "They did that this afternoon too."

"Really," Meg said softly.

DJ broke contact and rested his forehead against Becky's, softly whispering, "Their timing sucks."

"Mm," Becky hummed back, making him want to swallow her whole all over again.

"Geez. You guys go from zero to sixty in ten seconds," this voice belonged to Brooks.

DJ looked up to see his two siblings and their wives lined up in front of them. "That would be the pot calling the kettle black, don't ya think?"

Toni stood beside a new stroller, Brittany in her arms, and faced her husband. "He's got you there, dear."

Brooks moved forward. "Not the same at all. We had more than…"

"Four days," Adam tossed out.

Brooks frowned at his brother, then muffling a burst of laughter turned to Becky. "Welcome to the family."

EPILOGUE

E than swallowed another pain pill dry. The walls of his hospital room were closing in on him. When he finally got to the good doctors in country, they'd patched him up as best they could and the next day shipped him off to Germany. In Landstuhl, he'd undergone a second surgery and three days after that, he'd been on a C-17 back to the States and Walter Reed. More efficient than a Ford assembly line.

No longer on a morphine drip, Ethan had sputtered back to life from yet another surgery. At least they'd saved the leg. Now the question at hand—was it enough to save his career?

"No matter what, you can still fly as a civilian." Carter Jameson had been his roommate since arriving at Uncle Sam's five star medical facility.

Ethan resisted snapping back at the guy. He wasn't sure if the hospital had chosen Carter to be his bunkmate on purpose because the guy'd lost both his legs just below the knee or if it had simply been luck of the draw. Either way, it worked. Not that Ethan wasn't still mad as hell at the world and the damn Ground to Air Missiles that had sent his helo spiraling into the cold mountainside. But when the docs finally finished with him, Ethan would be walking out of rehab with the same two legs he'd been born with. A few extra screws and pins, but his legs.

"Mail call." An overly bouncy nurse came in and dropped a stack of letters in front of Ethan. "Don't see much snail mail anymore. And certainly not this soon. You're lucky."

"Yeah. Regular rabbit's foot," he mumbled to her back.

"Man," Carter pulled himself up with the overhead bars, staring at the letters, "you a Duggar or something?"

Another time and Ethan would have laughed. "Or something."

His aunt Eileen was a force to be reckoned with. The rest of the world had caught on to texts, emails, and computer calls, but his aunt still did paper and pen—every day.

Drugged and under the knife more often than he'd been awake and alert had kept him from receiving any outside news. Today was pretty much the first day he'd been lucid enough, and not quite as angry at the world, to even look at the communications from his family. And shit, they'd all gone off the deep end.

DJ alone had managed to shoot off what seemed like a thousand emails and private messages. His other brothers weren't far behind. The temptation to just select all and delete was quickly winning ground.

"You going to read them?" Carter asked, pointing with his chin at the stack Ethan had set aside on the bedside table.

"Yeah." In a minute. Shifting the angle of the bed, ignoring the hand written correspondence a while longer, using his good hand he clicked over to see what the family had been posting online lately. Straight off a pic of Adam and Meg with a couple of guests at her B&B made Ethan smile. Damn, he loved how happy that woman made Adam. More photos of each of his brothers and their new significant others took over the page. The women sure as hell took a lot more photos than the guys. A year ago he'd have been lucky to find a handful of pics on all the pages combined.

A rumble of laughter slipped out at a shot with little Stacey photo bombing her mom and Connor's carefully posed picture. He hadn't had a chance to meet her yet, but from what he'd heard and seen on the family's pages, he loved her already.

"Good news?" Carter asked.

Ethan nodded. He didn't want to lose the feeling of home that had taken over. Wasn't ready to go back to dealing with the reality of war. Scrolling down with his unbandaged hand, his fingers jerked off the keyboard. Becky stood beside DJ, she'd done something different to herself. Her hair? Makeup? Her clothes? That was it. He clicked on the photo to make it larger. Ethan didn't think he'd seen Becky in anything but jeans and scrubs for years.

"Wow." Still in jeans but this time with a form-fitting blouse that teased at a hint of cleavage, Ethan's eyes almost popped out of his head. Then he saw it. Not the blouse, or the figure, but the look. Her gaze was fixed on DJ and the damnedest thing, DJ was looking back at her with the same unswerving adoration that Ethan had come to recognize in Adam, Brooks and Connor. "Well, I'll be..." *DJ and Becky*.

Now eager to see what the heck was going on, he moved the cursor passing over the pics of his other brothers, ranch animals, and stopped at what had to be the Saturday poker game. All the social club ladies were there, as were his Dad and Finn. But it was DJ and Becky that had him grinning. Yep. Another one bites the dust. And Ethan couldn't be happier. Every single shot where he could see his brother and Becky, the two were attached at the hip. Some looking at each other like they couldn't hit the sheets fast enough. Wasn't that an odd thought. *Little Becky*. Ethan shook his head. Spunky and innocent Becky. He so wasn't going there.

Another shot of Brooks, Toni and someone's baby showed DJ in the background and the way he was staring off in the distance, Ethan would bet a year's pay that the beauty on the other end of that besotted gaze was Becky. Too funny.

More pics of smiling faces, happy couples, and the baby. The kid seemed to be passed around like a Monday night football. But it was the look on Aunt Eileen's face that had him studying the photo a little more closely. She looked way too enthralled with the infant. "What the?"

"Bad news?"

Ethan looked up to see a middle aged nurse with an artificially bright smile at his side and closed the window into his family's world. "No."

She nodded and shifted the blanket, poking and moving his toes. From where he lay, the exposed portion of his foot not swaddled in the cast resembled sausage stuffing overflowing from the snug skin. He wondered what his hand looked like beneath the thick bandage.

"Can you wiggle your toes for me?"

He did as instructed, although the maneuver didn't happen without a pain shooting up his leg.

"Swelling is improving," the attractive nurse informed him, directing her attention from his foot to his hand, "and I'll be changing the dressing on that next, but first can you wiggle your fingers as well?"

Not quite as swollen as his foot, his fingers moved stiffly, but thank God they moved.

"I'd say for a fellow who walked away from a crash—"

"Controlled crash," he corrected.

"A controlled crash, you're in pretty good shape. Very lucky."

There was that word again. Grounded for weeks of recovery and months of therapy, he felt anything but. "How long before I'm released?"

"You'll have to speak to Commander Billings. She should be making rounds soon."

Billings, the surgeon. Good looking, pretty face, nice smile when she used it. And even under the white coat he could tell she hid an A-1 figure. Another place and time and maybe…but not anymore. Except for Brooks, Ethan didn't want anything else to do with doctors. Especially one who might keep him from flying. All he wanted was out of this place and back in the cockpit, and if he never dealt with another doctor again as long as he lived, it would be too soon. Even one who looked like a bit of heaven on earth.

Enjoy an excerpt from

Ethan

"**C**lear to lift." Weeks of planning, coordinating, training until the team could have pulled this mission off in their sleep was about to pay off. Eight souls aboard and another pilot on their way home.

Out of nowhere shouts of "Missile, Missile, Missile" sounded in Ethan's headphones. Over his shoulder he caught the signature of the ground-to-air-missile. *Damn.* A kaleidoscope of orange and yellow flashed to his right and the helicopter rocked left. *Son of a...* The aircraft pitched up and down, then side to side. Not how he'd planned to end this mission. Using the intercom, he called for the other pilot to empty his weapons system, "Fire it out." Making a spiral descent, this bird was going down. Fast. *Crap.*

Surrounded by difficult terrain, the GPS, radio and emergency beacon probably wouldn't be worth a damn, and time was not on his side. Riding a pissed off bull with his nuts strapped was a piece of cake compared to controlling a helo with its tail boom severed. He had nine men on board. They'd come too damn far not to make it back to their families. *You go home with the one that brung ya.* Today was not a good day for these men to die. Ethan had brought 'em and he was taking 'em home.

The pounding repetition of gunfire blanketed them like the constant static crackling of a struggling comm system. Smoke seeped into the cockpit and the mountainside grew too damn close. "Not today," he muttered. Flames licked at his aircraft like a lizard trapping its prey. "Brace for impact!"

Ethan's eyes sprang open. *Breathe.* Calm. He was alive and... *not* hanging upside down. Blinking hard he glanced down at his hand. No shrapnel, no blood. A bandage. He blinked again and swallowed a hard gulp of calming air. "The men," he muttered before he remembered what was left of the helo had gotten all his passengers on the ground in mostly one piece.

"Are fine, Major." Commander Billings crossed the short

distance from the doorway to the bath and emerged with a wash cloth. Not saying a word, she dabbed away the sweat that had settled over his brow and trickled down his face. "I'm told what you did was nothing short of miraculous. Not many people survive helicopter crashes—"

"Controlled hard landing." He didn't want to hear the word crash again.

"Sorry. As I was saying, not many survive a hard landing, never mind an entire crew."

"How fine is fine?"

The pretty doctor frowned and then smiled again. "The other pilot is already patched up and back with your unit."

The fog in Ethan's brain continued to lift. He knew that. Knew his buddy Hammer was okay.

"The majority of the team are recovering from a range of broken bones, minor concussions and lacerations. A few first degree burns from getting everyone to safety. Lieutenant Bishop had to undergo surgery for a ruptured spleen along with internal bleeding, but he's recovering nicely."

Ethan knew that too. "You already told me this didn't you?"

The commander nodded. His forgetfulness must have been what had her frowning before, now she seemed pleased to have him remember. "You're progressing well. Foot looks good. Your hand too."

He wiggled his fingers and his toes. He wasn't sure how many days he'd been here, but he did know he was ready to get off his back. "How long before I return to duty?"

A single brow arched high on her forehead. "Marines," she muttered, softly shaking her head. "That's a serious break. You've had two surgeries and a nasty infection. Your bones need the same six to eight weeks to heal as mere mortal men."

Something about the way she teased made him relax. Reminded him of home. Now he remembered. He'd been looking at the computer, catching up, when he couldn't stay awake any longer. "My family?"

"Yes, well. It seems there was a bit of a paper glitch."

"Glitch?"

"They only received notice of your status yesterday. I understand your father and brother are on their way."

"No." If the doc was planning on keeping him on medical orders for two months, that meant he'd be going back to home station when released. In that case he might as well use up his accumulated leave and get his ass home. If he had to be laid up he'd rather do it on the ranch. Not that going back to Pendleton was a bad thing—it just wasn't home. "That's not necessary."

"The hell it's not." Sean Farraday strode into the room. Over six foot dressed in standard West Texas attire, jeans, button down shirt, first place rodeo buckle, well worn—and polished—boots and of course, his Stetson, the man was an imposing presence. And a bit of an anomaly in Washington D.C. "You're just lucky Aunt Eileen isn't here or she'd be hugging the stuffing out of you already."

Ethan began to chuckle and a pulling pain stabbed at his side.

"Bruised ribs," the doctor explained. He didn't remember that. Of course, he hadn't had anything to laugh about since arriving at Walter Reed. "I'm Commander Billings," she said as she extended her hand.

"How do you do?" His dad shook the offered hand. "You been taking good care of my boy?"

The woman's eyes twinkled with humor, but she had the decency not to laugh at Ethan being referred to as a boy. "We're all doing our best."

"Good." His father turned, a crease between his brow, and approached his son. "How you feeling really?"

"Like a swim in the creek. Should be nice and high about now."

His dad smiled. "Could be better."

"Not enough rain?" Not all of the brain fog from the post-surgery drugs had lifted. He should know the answer.

"Enough," Sean answered, studying his son from head to toe

as if he were a brand spanking newborn.

"So what's the other guy look like?" Slipping a phone into his pocket, DJ came into the room and stuck his hand out at the doctor who seemed a bit awestruck at a second six foot plus man in cowboy hat and boots. "I'm Declan."

"Declan?" Ethan muttered in surprise. "You in the doghouse?"

His dad shook his head, smiling. "Seems Becky thinks Declan is a nice name."

So he wasn't misinterpreting the internet posts. "I'll be…"

"If you'll excuse me." Dr. Billings stepped aside. "I have rounds to make. If you have any questions the nurse can page me, otherwise, your son should be on his way back to California any day."

DJ and their dad exchanged a quick sideways glance and Ethan didn't like the look of it. When he'd first discovered the barrage of contacts from his siblings he'd wondered what was up. Once he'd seen the doe-eyed photos of his brother and Becky, he'd figured that's what the messages were all about. The Farraday brothers were dropping like flies. At least he knew for sure not only was Becky a great catch, but he would kick his brother's sorry ass from here to Bagram if he let her down. But that look had nothing to do with lovesick sons.

"So what the hell is going on?"

MEET CHRIS

USA TODAY Bestselling Author of more than a dozen contemporary novels, including the award winning *Champagne Sisterhood*, Chris Keniston lives in suburban Dallas with her husband, two human children, and two canine children. Though she loves her puppies equally, she admits being especially attached to her German Shepherd rescue. After all, even dogs deserve a happily ever after.

More on Chris and her books can be found at
www.chriskeniston.com

Follow Chris on Facebook at ChrisKenistonAuthor
or on Twitter @ckenistonauthor

Questions? Comments?
I would love to hear from you.
You can reach me at chris@chriskeniston.com

Printed in Great Britain
by Amazon